I0557171

The Worst Man in the World by Edgar Wallace

Richard Horatio Edgar Wallace was born on the 1st April 1875 in Greenwich, London. Leaving school at 12 because of truancy, by the age of fifteen he had experience; selling newspapers, as a worker in a rubber factory, as a shoe shop assistant, as a milk delivery boy and as a ship's cook.

By 1894 he was engaged but broke it off to join the Infantry being posted to South Africa. He also changed his name to Edgar Wallace which he took from Lew Wallace, the author of Ben-Hur.

In Cape Town in 1898 he met Rudyard Kipling and was inspired to begin writing. His first collection of ballads, The Mission that Failed! was enough of a success that in 1899 he paid his way out of the armed forces in order to turn to writing full time.

By 1904 he had completed his first thriller, The Four Just Men. Since nobody would publish it he resorted to setting up his own publishing company which he called Tallis Press.

In 1911 his Congolese stories were published in a collection called Sanders of the River, which became a bestseller. He also started his own racing papers, Bibury's and R. E. Walton's Weekly, eventually buying his own racehorses and losing thousands gambling. A life of exceptionally high income was also mirrored with exceptionally large spending and debts.

Wallace now began to take his career as a fiction writer more seriously, signing with Hodder and Stoughton in 1921. He was marketed as the 'King of Thrillers' and they gave him the trademark image of a trilby, a cigarette holder and a yellow Rolls Royce. He was truly prolific, capable not only of producing a 70,000 word novel in three days but of doing three novels in a row in such a manner. It was estimated that by 1928 one in four books being read was written by Wallace, for alongside his famous thrillers he wrote variously in other genres, including science fiction, non-fiction accounts of WWI which amounted to ten volumes and screen plays. Eventually he would reach the remarkable total of 170 novels, 18 stage plays and 957 short stories.

Wallace became chairman of the Press Club which to this day holds an annual Edgar Wallace Award, rewarding 'excellence in writing'.

Diagnosed with diabetes his health deteriorated and he soon entered a coma and died of his condition and double pneumonia on the 7th of February 1932 in North Maple Drive, Beverly Hills. He was buried near his home in England at Chalklands, Bourne End, in Buckinghamshire.

Index of Contents
I - The First Crime
II - The Snake Woman
III - On the Cornish Express
IV - The Master Criminal
V - The House of Doom
VI - The Last Crime
Edgar Wallace – A Short Biography

Edgar Wallace – A Concise Bibliography

Although these experiences are told in story form, they represent the personal narrative of one who served many terms of penal servitude, and were related to the author, who met with this remarkable convict a few days after his last release from prison.

I

THE FIRST CRIME

When I left Dartmoor prison some seven years ago, the Deputy saw me in the governor's pokey little office hung around with the art exhibits of former convicts.

"Smith," he said, "I suppose there is no use my saying that I hope I shall never see you here again?"

"No, sir," said I. "I should hate to disappoint you, and the chances are that I shall be back in a year or two. I used to under-rate the intelligence of Scotland Yard, but my views have undergone a change."

The Deputy laughed.

"I think you're the worst man in the world," he said, "because you commit crimes deliberately, and it seems to me that you have as deliberately chosen your career; I have never known another prisoner who has cold-bloodedly set himself to go wrong as you have. And yet you were a gentleman, you have education and natural gifts, and you can't go straight."

"I can go straight, sir, but I don't," said I.

We walked up the sloping hill to the big steel gates, and I stepped out into the space before the guard-room.

"I was reading up your record yesterday," he said. "You have been in prison six times. You have been flogged and punished in other ways, and yet none of these things have a deterrent effect upon you. I am afraid that one of these days you'll toe the chalk line."

"That I shall never do," said I, for if he had but known, the only thing I ever saw in prison which filled me with fear was that little T drawn in chalk on the trap of the scaffold where a condemned man puts his feet.

And sitting in my little bungalow on the Sussex shore, with a somewhat adventurous life behind me, and no further desire or need for going on the dodge, I think it is unlikely that I shall ever be hanged. For murder is a cheap and cowardly business, and I do not think it is in me to commit so beastly a crime, even if I had not helped strip a few men who had been "hanged by the neck until they were dead."

Executions have always put the wind up me, and I've never known anybody who was so callous that they were not affected. I have seen a hangman reeling along the exercise ground drunk with the horror of his job, and I have looked one famous young killer of men in the eyes—one of the Billingtons had hanged twenty-one men before his twenty-first birthday!—and read the gloomy terror of his soul.

And I have known a warder who went white in twenty-four hours. There was a man hanged in a northern gaol, and the fellow was a brute. He tried to kill one of the warders in charge, the man I am speaking about, and spent the last three days of his life in a straight-jacket.

And as the procession formed up, and he came out of his cell, he turned to the warder and said:

"I hate you! I'll hate you after I'm dead!"

And when the drop fell, and the man was undoubtedly past all knowledge of life, he seemed to shake his upturned face—masked as it was with the linen "cap"—at the horrified warder as he gazed down.

And now let me begin the somewhat uninteresting preamble to the story of my life.

For the past three months I have been wallowing in criminal apologia. In other words, I have been reading the very many volumes which have been constructed by eminent criminals who were sufficiently in the public eye at the time of their conviction to justify enterprising editors in securing their reminiscences.

They are unconsciously humorous, these recollections, for they are apparently written by white-souled creatures, who committed no crime, and who were quite innocent of the charges brought against them. Not a small portion of these volumes, varying in size and importance from library editions to paper-backed, ill-printed sixpenny brochures, is devoted to an indignant refutation of the charges which brought them into penal servitude. They "never done it"—it was always the other fellow.

The writers contribute nothing to the world's knowledge of the criminal classes, and precious little to our faith in humanity. Their books and recollections are hypocritical twaddle, sometimes amusing, more often sickening, and in more cases than one these wretched autobiographies are employed as a peg upon which to hang charges against the unhappy officials who do their best, and their honest best, to administer the law.

In four cases out of five the autobiographies are written up by professional writers who introduce their own elegant language somewhat incongruously.

The remarkable thing about these recollections of mine is that they are recollections of an admitted criminal, and a man who takes pride in the fact that he was never adequately punished for his breaches of the law, and who recalls with a complacent satisfaction that, despite the punishment which he has undergone, he has missed that which, if every man had his due, would have been his in addition.

Since most of the volumes of reminiscences start with a genealogical-tree, and an exposition of the respectability of the writer's forbears, I will be so far conventional as to say that my father was a very excellent man. He was, in fact, a peer of the realm, which seems a somewhat melodramatic and unconvincing claim, but it is one which must be made because it is the truth. My brother was and my nephew is the present holder of the title, and it is a queer fact that had my nephew died in France—as he nearly did—I should have been "my lord." Happily he lives and has, I hope, many years of vigorous life before him,

I was educated at a famous school, which it will serve no useful purpose to mention, and at a military school, whence I was gazetted to the first cavalry regiment which left these shores for South Africa after the outbreak of war. I do not purpose giving you the story of my adventures in South Africa, but it is sufficient to say that I made a fool of myself over a woman in Cape Town, had a row with the senior major of my regiment, and another row with yet another superior, and was out of the Army before the war had comfortably settled down.

I came home, and was received by my male parent at Southampton. We had lunch, and he was as nice as the circumstances allowed. He explained to me that he was not a very rich man, but I was the first of the family who had ever disgraced his name. He thanked his Maker that my mother was dead, and said most of the things that a man with a limited vocabulary and a dearth of original ideas would say under the circumstances. He wound up with a suggestion that I should go back to South Africa, join the South African Light Horse as a trooper, and extinguish myself in a blaze of glory.

I thought it was a good idea, and it was certainly advice which I should have passed on to somebody else, but so far as I was concerned it did not raise so much as a thrill. I told him so.

The upshot was that he gave me £500 and told me to go to hell. Those were his exact words.

I suppose that I should say here that I have been through many brands of hell since that beautiful morning in June, 1901. But if I said that I should be a hypocrite, too, for hell is only the unendurable and the unimaginable, and my worst experiences have deserved neither of these descriptions.

I left Southampton by the night boat for Havre, and gravitated to Paris. I had been there three days when I got into a row at one of the night-places. The row ended in my arrest and my being fined, and I was instructed to leave Paris as soon as possible.

I left France by way of Monte Carlo and the Riviera and I was back again in England on September 13th, 1901, arriving in London with exactly four shillings and tuppence-halfpenny, a five-franc piece, and no immediate prospects of making a decent living with a minimum of hard labour.

It was here, at Charing Cross railway station at half-past eleven o'clock at night, that I resolved to be a criminal. I reached this decision calmly and deliberately. After all, I come from a long line of criminals. The founder of my house was a robber who stole land, the reviver of our ancestral glories was a woman who was a very close friend indeed of one of the Stuart princes.

It is true that very few men resolve upon a career which involves a total disregard for the law. Men drift into crime as, with more happy results, other men drift into other professions. It is largely a matter of early training and environment. What are known as the "criminal classes" are people whose natural and instinctive predatory impulses are unchecked by discipline. Every babe is born into the world a conscienceless thief, and is taught by nurses and mother, by schoolmaster and father, and, finally, by an appreciation of the law's true majesty that of all the goods in the world only a very few are his, and even those must be consumed or employed in accordance with the ritual of behaviour.

The idea which is behind all the Prisoners' Aid Societies and the like, that crime is the phenomenon of good people becoming suddenly bad people, and the further absurd belief that these suddenly bad people can be turned back into good people is as fallacious as would be the suggestion that a snub nose can be converted into a Roman nose on the impulse of a moment.

This digression is by-the-way. I was in London. I was broke. I had no desire to "work," because work implied a fixity of habit and a certain drab sameness of existence. I declare to-day that I regard prison life as infinitely more satisfying to the romantic soul than the most comfortable of Government jobs. In prison a man of culture and imagination cannot stagnate nor be content with his lot. If it is only the ambition to be a free man he at least is the possessor of aspirations. Moreover, he dreams, and that is very blessed.

I drove to an hotel in the City, and was shown to a dull and gloomy room, uglier than any of those bright and cheery apartments in which delinquency is stored for recuperation and renewal. And I remember I sat until the day broke puzzling out how best I could begin.

Has this ever struck you—that for hundreds of years architects, tailors, builders of all kinds, iron-masters and the like, have devoted their best energies to the frustrating of thieves! The dominant note of civilisation is suspicion. Billions of money have been spent not only to induce mankind to the paths of virtue but to take jolly good care that it did not stray. The first essential of all houses is that none shall be able to enter except authorised persons. The steel-makers produce bars for the windows and locks for the doors. The tailor contrives cunning pockets which cannot be picked. Corporations have been formed to keep the loose cash of the community in safe keeping—it seems that the first essential of manufacture shall be security against the thief.

All night long I planned and thought, and always I came up against locks, bolts, and bars.

I had—and have still—a sister; she is a woman of the low intelligence which is peculiar to her class. A hard, mercenary, ungentle woman, she married a worthy mate in a long-faced prig who collected china and wrote wearisome articles in the dull reviews. They had a house in Portman Square, at which I have dined just as often as I had to. It was a house very near to one at which King Edward was a frequent visitor. John X., my brother-in-law, had, I knew, one peculiarity. He always kept a reserve fund of a thousand pounds in the house. I cannot exactly remember what was the reason he offered for this eccentricity, but I have a vague idea—and this, I admit,

I may have unconsciously invented—that he once found himself without money after banking hours on a Saturday when an emergency arose calling for his immediate departure for the Continent.

I lay down on my bed at five o'clock in the morning with my object well defined. My plan, however, was more or less nebulous. I made a survey of the house the following afternoon. It backed on to a mews, and there was a door communicating with a small yard, a door which apparently was used by tradesmen. Usually, even in big London houses, tradesmen go to the front, descending a flight of steps to the area-kitchen entrance.

Whilst I was examining the front of the house a victoria drove up, and my sister and brother-in-law descended. They went into the house, and immediately afterwards another carriage pulled up, and this time a man got-out assisted by a footman. He had something the matter with his leg, and had to be assisted up the steps by the footman, who came down to meet him. Evidently he was some friend of

John's. I came nearer to the door the better to see, for as the footman took the visitor along the hall he left the door wide open. Here was a chance, and on the impulse of the moment I took it. I walked casually up the steps and through the open door. I was well-dressed, and I looked a gentleman, and I could always find an excuse for entering the wrong house if the servant spotted me. But he didn't. The lame man's arm was round his neck, obstructing his view, and his back was towards me as he helped the man into what I knew was John's library.

I passed the open door of this room and ran quickly up the carpeted stairs. My real danger was that I might meet one of the servants, or John and Millicent, but there was nobody in sight. The first floor consisted of a drawing-room and Millicent's sitting-room. At the back was the housekeeper's room, and another apartment where the family sometimes breakfasted.

On the next floor were the principal bed- and dressing-rooms, a sort of study where John burned the midnight current over his review articles, and a sort of conservatory built out on a balcony at the back of the house. I heard voices above, and recognised one as Millicent's. The other was evidently a maid. Millicent is a representative of that old nobility which expresses its patrician qualities by making the lives of servants a burden. I turned into the side passage, which I knew led to the housekeeper's room. It was any odds against old Mrs. Fenny—which is not her name—being in her room when Millicent was rampaging around.

And here my luck was with me. The door was locked from the outside, but the key was in the lock. The room was not only empty, but on the one table of the room were a number of lists and three bunches of keys. The door of the wardrobe was open, and there was not a single article of clothing in the room. I guessed at once that Millicent was without a housekeeper. The poor old lady had probably been fired (I learnt afterwards that the housekeeper I had known had been dead for three years, and that it was the second of her successors, a young and attractive woman, who had been turned out, for reasons which I need not give).

The wardrobe was a big, old-fashioned affair which might, in a moment of emergency, become a useful hiding-place, but I guessed that the room itself would be all the hiding-place I wanted. I opened the door cautiously, took out the key and locked the door from the inside. Then I went to the window and had a good look round. The window faced the mews, and outside was a flat, lead-covered roof about ten feet square. I didn't know, nor do I know now, what room it covered, but it seemed a fairly easy way out of the house if I were pressed, or if somebody tried to enter the room. But nobody did. I sat in that infernal bedroom from three o'clock in the afternoon until eight o'clock at night and I was famished. There was not even a glass of water. I had taken off my shoes and had put them in my two pockets, and most of the time I spent sitting near the door on a chair, listening.

The only clue I had as to the family movements was when I heard John say, evidently answering some inquiry which had been fired down the stairs by Millicent:

"Balfour says he will look in, but that will rather crowd the box."

Which was very good news. For it told me they were going to a theatre. It was nine o'clock when I ventured forth. Happily my sister is an economical soul, and insisted upon all unnecessary lights being extinguished even when she was in the house. The hall below was dimly illuminated, and there was only one light on each landing, and those fairly dim. There was no sound or movement when I walked up the stairs. The servants would be in the kitchen, I thought, though I was mistaken. I had reached the upper landing when I heard a door close at the end of a passage corresponding to that which led to the housekeeper's room on the floor below. I opened the first door handy, and slipped in. The room was in darkness, but I saw that I was in Millicent's bedroom. Owing to the carpet on the landing and stairs I heard nothing more. After ten minutes' waiting I went out again into the passage and made for John's bedroom and study. The bedroom was easily entered, but the door leading to his study was locked. I went again to the passage and listened. Presently from down below came the slam of a door. If that meant that the person I had heard had gone below to the servants hall I could take a risk. I put on the lights and explored the room, and found the key in a drawer of John's dressing-table. A few seconds later I was in the study. I had been in this room before once in my life, and I knew that John kept his reserve in an oaken cupboard.

If I give an account of my first crime in detail it is because every incident of that exciting night is stamped on my memory. But I will spare the reader of these notes a description of the horrible hour and a half I spent over that infernal cupboard. If John had had a safe like a rational being I should have given up my attempt at once. As it was I went to work, and hot work it was. The cupboard was set in the wall. It was an old-fashioned affair, but an expert burglar with a kit of tools would have had the door open in five minutes. After some consideration I hit upon this method. There was a coal-fire laid in the study, and this I kindled. It was half-an hour before I could heat the poker sufficiently, but when I did I began to bore a hole through the door. It was another hour before the hole was big enough to put my hand through, and by that time the room was thick with smoke and reeking of scorched wood. My danger was that the smell of the burning would reach the hall, and I was a bit rattled at the thought.

At the end of what seemed hours—I had my watch open on a chair beside me—I got my hand in and found the tin box where the money was kept. The box was too big to pull through the hole, and if it had been locked John would have saved his money, and his reputation would not have been imperilled. But it was not locked. It was filled with paper, and I dragged out handfuls of letters before I came to the nice, crepe-silky feeling banknotes. There were sixty-three notes for a hundred pounds, and I slipped them into my pocket. The letters I glanced at. They were from a lady, and really I was tempted to put them under Millicent's pillow. John I knew as a prig. I never suspected him of being such a smug hypocrite. I only half read one letter, and chucked the rest on to the fire. I washed my hands and dried them in John's bedroom, and then, pulling on my shoes, I opened the door and stepped out into the passage—face to face with a servant girl!

She saw me and gave a yell, then flew down the stairs screaming at the top of her voice.

I only hesitated a moment, then ran down after her. I had not reached the first landing when I heard a man's voice immediately below, and, turning, ran up the stairs. The top floor was the fourth, and consisted of servant's attics. I ran into one, shut and locked the door behind me, for my pursuer was at my heels. As to one thing I was determined. I would not reveal my relationship with John or Millicent even to them. Not because I wanted to save the family name or any nonsense of that kind, but because I knew that John would prosecute and I did not want the additional publicity. An ordinary burglar would get a few lines in the papers and pass out of the public mind, a "lordly burglar"—I can imagine the headlines!—would be a marked man.

The servant's room was an attic. Outside the open window, as I had seen, was a parapet. I got through the window and ran along the stone coping, which extended for the width of three houses. Then I dropped about eight feet to the flat roof of another house, crossed the roof to where the top rungs of a fire-escape showed even in the darkness, and went down until I found myself on a narrow balcony.

There was a big window, which was open a little at the top, and I lifted the bottom sash without any difficulty and stepped in. The room was dark, but I had hardly put my foot upon the floor when it was brilliantly illuminated.

I was in a beautiful bedroom, and, unfortunately, it was occupied.

Sitting up in bed, staring at me with a white face, was the most beautiful girl I had ever seen.

"What do you want?" she gasped.

"I'm a detective," I said. "I'm after a burglar who has got into your house."

I didn't wait for any further explanation. I was through the door and down the stairs in a few seconds. Fortunately for me, I met not a soul. The front door was chained and locked, but I got it open and was in the street in time to see two policeman going up the steps of John's house.

II

THE SNAKE WOMAN

I always think and speak of her as the Snake Woman, although there was little about her that was snake-like. Reading this, as she may, she will think my description an uncomplimentary one; but you shall judge if it is just.

The most amazing thing about the Snake Woman is this: that only two years ago an American of German or Scandinavian descent committed exactly the crime which the Snake Woman planned!

I met her after my third—or, it may be, my fourth—job.

One of the first crimes I committed required all the nerve and resourcefulness of an experienced criminal, and had I known the difficulties which would beset me, I certainly would have tried some easier method of acquiring wealth.

It was nothing less picturesque than a Hatton Garden robbery, which involved the breaking into an office and the opening of a steel safe. I got into the office easily enough, for I had made friends with one of the clerks, whom I met at a music-hall—I had no idea of robbing his employer until he told me where he was working—and, by pretending to be interested in the methods which are employed to prevent burglaries, I succeeded in getting from him minute particulars of how Mr. Bernstein—that was not the name of the eminent dealer in precious stones—guarded his treasures.

The result was a haul of ninety-six diamonds, half of which were uncut, which I afterwards sold in Amsterdam much below their value; but this haul had its drawbacks. The young clerk told the police all about the well-dressed stranger who had made the inquiries, and gave so faithful a description of me that, even though I shaved off my moustache and adopted a pair of spectacles and a studious look, I had an uneasy feeling that every policeman whom I passed was looking at me suspiciously.

The consequence was that when I was eventually arrested—taken red-handed breaking into a jeweller's shop through the skylight—why do jewellers always have skylights?—the youth came up and recognised me, and my first introduction to one of his Majesty's judges resulted in my being sent to penal servitude for five years. Five years for a first conviction was rather thick, but, of course, it was no more than I deserved. Happily, I had cached about five hundred pounds at a suburban branch of a well-known bank, and had been sufficiently shrewd not to take a cheque-book or passbook from the banker; so that when the police searched my belongings there was nothing to indicate that I was a man of wealth and position.

I shall never forget my first introduction to Wormwood Scrubs, and I must confess that I was agreeably surprised at the cleanliness and the rough comfort of prison life. An ordinary prisoner, in spite of what the cinema pictures tell you, does not wear knee-breeches and grey stockings, with broad arrows stuck all over him. He wears a stout, brown pair of trousers, a waistcoat and a coat of the same material, a blue and white shirt, and a queer little hat. Even when he is transferred—I am talking of the present time—to Dartmoor he does not acquire grey stockings.

I was doing hard work, but not too hard. The food was coarse, but wholesome, and I really didn't feel as depressed as I might have done, realising that I should be out again in three and a half years if I behaved myself.

In three months' time I was put on a train at Paddington with six or seven other unfortunate gentlemen, and despatched to Dartmoor. We were chained together, and I do not think that my most intimate friend would have recognised the unshaven young man who stood at the head of the chained gang as the some-time officer of a crack cavalry corps.

It was a long and tedious journey before we reached Princetown, but at Dartmoor one felt, for some extraordinary reason, tremendously at home. The moment I left Princetown Station I realised that I was amongst friends. People did not stare at us; they regarded us as part of the natural scenery, I suppose.

In Dartmoor I was placed in B Ward. I remember marching up from the station, passing under that grim arch with its grimmer jest carved in its granite face, and halting before the great steel grille that led into the prison proper, whilst the head warder checked us over before he turned the big key in the gun-metal lock and the gate swung open to admit us to what has been picturesquely described as a living hell, but which, in reality, is not half as bad as it is painted. I admit, of course, that it is bitterly cold in the winter; but Dartmoor was one of the first prisons to adopt central heating, and though it is old and smelly, and should be pulled down and replaced by modern buildings, it is one of the most comfortable prisons I have ever been in. Its cells are large, light, and airy, the food is good, and the discipline, though strict, is not oppressive.

The second impression was the depth of the recesses in which the cell doors stood, and the narrowness of those yellow doors. They do not appear very formidable, those doors, with their little ventilators; you feel that with a good kick you could break them in. I have often wondered how they got the Tichborne claimant through those narrow entrances. (I have seen the lasts of his boots in the cobbler's shop scores of times, and it is one of the things they pull out to show visitors.)

As I have said before, I have read most of the memoirs of distinguished prisoners, but from none of these do I receive an exact impression of Dartmoor. Most of the writers, being "innocent," are obsessed with their grievances, and they seem surprised that the warders and officials of the prison did not share their illusions.

The Snake Woman came into my life a few months before I had completed my sentence.

As my term of imprisonment was nearly at an end, and as, moreover, I had got into the star class by my good conduct—and it is the easiest thing in the world to be well conducted in gaol—I was allowed a certain liberty of action. I had only worked for a few weeks in the field, and I had not been in the quarry at all.

One afternoon I was sent to paint a barn situated about a quarter of a mile from the gaol, and although, officially, I was under the care of a warder, I was in point of fact my own master. I carried the paint-pot up the road, and was turning into the field where the barn was situated, when I heard the sound of a horse's galloping feet behind me, and looked over my shoulder.

It was a woman, and she was riding astride, which was rather unusual in those days. I turned my head to the front, and heard the horse approach closer and closer. Presently it fell into a walk, and just as my hand was on the gate the rider came abreast.

"Man," said a low voice.

I looked back. It was a pretty face I saw, hard, but pretty. My memory is of level eyebrows and two big dark eyes that seemed to search my soul.

"You will get into trouble," I said in as low a voice as hers, "if you are seen speaking with a convict."

"When will you be released from gaol?" she asked, to my surprise.

"In May, the fourteenth to be exact," I answered.

"What is your name?" she asked hastily. "Where can I find you? I have a job for you that may give you enough money to start you in life."

Her question knocked me out, and I was very anxious to end the interview, if for no other reason than that I did not want to be seen speaking to a member of the public, an indiscretion on my part which would cost me many marks and a cancellation of my remission of sentence.

"Write to John Smith, c.o. Aylesbury, Newsagent, Castle Street, Pimlico," I said, giving her the name and address which I had used for my erratic correspondence.

She repeated the words in a low voice, and then, touching the horse with her heels, she moved off. Only just in time, for that minute a warder came round the corner of the road.

"Did you speak to that lady?" he asked.

"Yes, sir," I replied. "She asked me which was the Tavistock Road, and I told her that she must not speak to a prisoner."

"She spoke to you first, did she?" he asked suspiciously, and looked as though he would have liked to have called the lady back, to be certain that I had not annoyed her, though Heaven knows, very few prisoners who are allowed out of gaol are ever guilty of such impertinence.

At any rate, the lady was now cantering, and was too far off to be called back, and the "screw" seemed satisfied, for he told me to go to my job.

About two hours afterwards, when he came to collect me, to march me back to the working party, he said:

"That lady is staying in Princetown at the Duchess Hotel; it is queer that she didn't know the way to Tavistock."

"That is what I thought, sir," said I; and there the matter ended.

Immediately on my release from prison I made for London. I confess that, although I had given this strange woman an occasional thought, I had not taken any very serious notice of her remarkable introduction to me, deciding in my mind that, moved to pity by what she thought my unfortunate circumstances, she had impulsively decided to give me a hand to lead a better life.

I never expected to hear from her, and I was amazed when I made my call that same evening at the little shop in Pimlico where my letters were addressed, to find one written in a strange but feminine hand, addressed to Mr. Smith, and not only marked "Private," but heavily sealed.

My curiosity was immediately aroused, and at the first opportunity I tore open the flap and extracted a heavy and expensive sheet of notepaper which bore no address or signature. It ran:

"When you receive this, please put an advertisement in the agony column of 'The Times,' saying 'Will meet you at nine o'clock to-night near the Magazine, Hyde Park.' I shall be wearing a black costume and a veil."

The spirit of adventure is never stronger in a man than on the day he is released from prison. The theory that prison crushes a man's spirit is all bunkum. I needed no second telling. And by great good luck, I was in time to get an advertisement in "The Times" that night, and it appeared the following morning.

At nine o'clock, just as it was getting dark, I made my way to that part of Hyde Park where the Powder Magazine is situated. A slight drizzle of rain was falling, and the pathways and seats were deserted. I had not been there three minutes before I saw a woman in a long black raincoat coming toward me, and as she neared me I saw that she was veiled. She had half passed me when she turned.

"Oh, it is you," she said. Her voice was low and musical, and I know it at once. "I should not have recognised you now that you are shaven," she said.

I fell in by her side as she crossed the road and made for one of the paths which stretch across the Park.

"What were you in prison for?"

"Burglary," said I.

I heard her utter an exclamation, and I had a curious sense that she was pleased to hear of my crime. A few seconds later she set any doubt I might have on that subject at rest.

"I am glad," she avid. "Have you been in prison before?"

"No," I confessed.

"And I suppose now you are going to lead an honest and upright life?"

I detected the irony in her tone. It amounted almost to a sneer.

"I am sorry to disappoint you," said I, "but I have no such intention. I shall make an heroic effort to keep out of prison, because Dartmoor, with all its advantages, is a little dull."

She said nothing, and we paced slowly in silence across that desolate stretch of grassland, as the rain pattered down in a hesitating way as though the clouds had not yet decided whether they would let their volumes loose upon the earth, or carry them to a land which was in greater need of humidity than ours.

"There are two chairs under that tree, I think," she said, stepping over the border, and walking across the grass. "We can talk there; there is nobody about to-night, thank goodness."

I put a chair for her, and sat by her side.

"Now, Mr. Smith—I suppose 'Smith' is not your name, but that doesn't matter—-I am going to tell you what I want you to do. I want you to commit a burglary."

I gaped at her.

"You're not serious?" I asked.

"I was never more serious in my life," she said earnestly. "Though it isn't exactly a burglary that I want you to commit. My husband, who is many years older than myself, is constantly making fun of me because of my dread of burglars. He says that nobody would ever dare to break into our house in Langdon Square, and my object in seeing you is to induce you to convince him he is wrong."

I was puzzled, and showed it.

"I don't quite see why you should take all this trouble," said I. "You mean, of course, you want a fake burglary?"

She nodded.

"I have taken the trouble, Mr. Smith," she said quietly, "because it is very important to me that my husband should not leave me alone so frequently, knowing, as he does, my terror of burglars."

"You are not exactly showing your terror of burglars at this precise moment," said I, with a smile. "Now, tell me, where do I come in in this matter?"

"You mean, how much will I pay you?" she asked quickly.

"No, no! I am not so mercenary as that. Am I to appear in the dead of night in your husband's bedroom?"

"I will pay you five hundred pounds," she said. "Let us settle that matter now. I will arrange for you to enter the house by the kitchen door, which I will leave ajar. You will make your way up to the first floor and hide yourself in the drawing-room, behind the screen which I will have placed for you. I shall be dining with my husband at the time, and shall bring him up to the room. When I cough twice, you are to come from your place of concealment and cry 'Hands up!'"

"Oh!" said I cautiously. "Am I to be armed?"

"Of course you are to be armed!" she said impatiently. "I want you to look like a burglar. You ought to wear a mask and have a revolver. Here it is."

She put her hand in the fold of her dress and took out a neat little Browning,

"It is loaded," she went on, but the safety-catch is down."

"And then what happens?" I asked curiously.

I guessed rather than saw the grimace she made. Evidently there was no love lost between herself and her elderly husband.

"I expect he will faint," she said drily, "and you will make your escape. I will arrange that all the servants, except the parlour-maid and the cook, are out of the house, and you will have no difficulty in making your way to safety. You are not afraid, are you?" she asked sarcastically.

"Not at all, madam," said I. "But it seems to me to be an extraordinary job. Do I get paid—"

"You get paid on the night," she said. "Behind the screen, on a little table, I will leave a pocket-book containing the money. You will put it in your pocket, and there will be an end to the adventure. Will you do it?"

I hesitated. It seemed a strange commission, and, candidly, I did not like it, the reason for my dislike being the necessity for carrying a loaded pistol into a dwelling-house, for the punishment meted out to the armed burglar is infinitely more drastic than to the burglar who is unarmed. Still, five hundred pounds was five hundred pounds, and it was not my business to question the lady's good taste or wifely affection.

"I'll do it," I said.

I have called her "a snake woman," and it was at that very moment that I got that snaky impression. It was not the undulation of her fine figure as she rose to her feet, nor her stealthy movement as she crossed to the path by my side, nor yet the hint of those fascinating eyes of hers which I had seen when she raised her veil. All I know is that a thrill ran down my spine, and it was some time before I could shake off the unpleasant feeling which her presence created.

She left me in the middle of the path, after giving her final directions, and I followed her at a distance, until I saw her enter a car near the bridge and drive away.

My first business was to find out who lived at No. 609, Langdon Square. I found it was Mr. and Lady Mary Krain. Krain was a City man, and his name was well-known to me. During the war he was, I believe, under suspicion, because of his German origin, but apparently he was sufficiently a patriot to escape any more unpleasant consequences.

Wednesday night was the time arranged, and at twenty minutes past nine I walked down the area steps of No. 609 and pushed at the kitchen door. It was open, and I entered, closing the door softly behind me. I was in a long passage which ran parallel with the kitchen, and terminated in a flight of stairs leading up into the hall. Her ladyship had laid her plans very carefully. Neither the cook nor the parlour maid nor any other servant was in sight, and a very dim light burnt in the hall, and I went up the stairs and into the drawing-room, which was illuminated by one electric globe.

It was a handsome drawing-room, furnished in that costly fashion which only the vulgarly rich can bring themselves to perpetrate. There was the screen. I stepped behind, and found a tiny table on which was a pocket-book. I opened the book, took out five hundred-pound notes, replaced them, and put the book in my pocket. Then I fixed my mask, and was preparing to wait, when it struck me that it would not be a bad idea if I made a reconnaissance of the room in case my way of retreat was barred.

There were three long French, windows opening on to a balcony, and if the worst came to the worst, there was an easy escape into the street. And then I was walking back to my place of concealment, after listening at the door, when on a round mahogany table, I saw what appeared to be a square of silk as though it were flung there by a careless hand. I put my hand on it, and felt something hard beneath. It was a Browning pistol! And it was loaded. I stood there for a minute, trying to piece together the scheme at the back of the lady's mind, and then I began to see daylight. Quickly I slipped down the magazine, emptied the cartridges into my hand and put them into my pocket; then I carefully drew back the bolt and extracted the one remaining cartridge which was in the chamber. This done, I replaced the pistol where it had been, under the square of green silk.

I had hardly done so when I heard voices on the stairs, and stepped noiselessly back to my place behind the screen. The door was opened, there was a flood of light, and I heard a man's complaining voice asking why any light at all had been left on in the drawing-room.

Between the frames of the screen I had a glimpse of a stout, bald man with a grey-black moustache. He was in evening-dress, and in his shirt sparkled a diamond of immense value. Behind him was the Snake Woman, and now I felt that my description of her was justified. She wore a tight-fitting dress of velvet, innocent of any embroidery and cut low before and behind. The only jewel she displayed was an emerald brooch pinned across her breast; her black hair fall in two waves, framing a white and aesthetic face that emphasised the darkness of those glowing eyes of hers.

"There's another thing," said Mr. Krain, as though he were continuing a conversation; "I will not have that man Thurgood here. I have told you about this before, Mary. I will not have it! The man makes love to you, the servants are talking, and although I take no notice of servants, I am not going to be made a laughing-stock. If you want a young man to love you, wait till I'm dead." He chuckled. "That'll be a good twenty years yet, my dear, and you won't be so attractive then."

"How dare you!" Her voice was vibrant with passion. "To insult me before—"

"Before whom?" asked Mr. Krain contemptuously; and then in a more kindly voice, he went on, "Drop him, Mary; he's a waster. No good can come out of it."

"Indeed!" she said coldly; and I saw her move to the table and her hand creep under the silk. "Let me be the beat judge of that."

She coughed twice.

"Have you got a cold?" asked Krain, peering round at her through his spectacles.

It was at that moment I made my dramatic appearance. My mask on my face, a pistol in my hand, I must have been a terrifying object.

"Hands up!" I said.

He spun round, his face pallid.

"What—what!" he stammered, and then I saw the thing which I expected. The Snake Woman took deliberate aim at him, and pressed the trigger. There was a click, and she stared aghast.

Krain was looking at me. He had not seen what she had done.

"I have taken the liberty of unloading your pistol, Lady Mary," said I, as I made for the door. "Don't move! My pistol is loaded, and I shall have no hesitation in sending you where you intended sending me. If you make a noise, I'll tell the truth. Do you understand that?"

I slipped through the door, closed it behind me, and in a few seconds was in the street. At the corner stood a policeman, and I bade him a cheery good-night as I strode past, both my hands in my overcoat pockets, one gripping a black mask, the other a ten-shotted pistol.

The Snake Woman was clever, but not as clever as she might have been. She intended killing her husband, and then shooting me. She had brought me there for the purpose. Her story would have been that she was surprised by a burglar, a man with a criminal record who had recently come out of Dartmoor, and that the burglar had shot her husband, and that she, in turn, had shot the burglar in self-defence. Who would doubt the word of Lady Mary against an ex-convict? It was a pretty plan. I remembered it some three years later, when I strolled into the Divorce Court and heard the undefended petition of Mr. Krain.

The average warder is neither brutal nor tyrannous; he is a very human individual, poorly paid, and in consequence recruited from the same class as you recruit your army. Often he is an old soldier, with all an old soldier's dislike for hard work. He lives all the time in fear of the "half-sheet"—in other words, the complaint that brings him before the governor, and when you realise that a complaint of any prisoner must be investigated, and if there is the slightest ground for such complaint the warder gets a telling-off, you can understand that a warder's life is a dog's life.

I would personally sooner be a thief, because a thief is sometimes out of prison, and at the worst, if I am captured, and sent to a long term of penal servitude, I can only be reduced to the same sordid surroundings, the same wretched atmosphere, as the honest warder endures.

I am not going to attempt, in this short biography, to engage in the heart-breaking task of prison reform, My own opinion is that prisoners, particularly short-term prisoners, are treated a jolly sight too well; but what did always amuse me was the star prisoner. Men are placed in a certain class, and because they are so promoted there is a prevalent idea that they are less liable to the contamination of their companions. It is rather like putting a man in a special kind of jacket and turning him loose amongst small-pox patients, telling him that because he is wearing a blue coat he will not be infected!

Are crimes hatched in prison? I suppose they are. Men in the solitude of their cells think out new schemes of getting easy money, and usually take some prison friend into their confidence. A prison friendship is very much like ship-board friendship: it is very violent whilst you are in prison, but it peters out the moment you are free. The average lag is a criminal and nothing will reform him; he is a man of low mentality, and very often on the border line of imbecility. You have only to see the faces of the men who are constantly and continually in prison to realise that crime is a disease with them, and invariably the criminal is created by hereditary influences. His father and mother have bequeathed to him a weakness of resistance, an inability to reason logically, and the basis of all crimes, with rare exceptions, of which I am an exponent, is the inability to prevision the effects which follow causes.

Thirty per cent. of habitual criminals should be in lunatic asylums, which really means that they should be placed in a lethal chamber and destroyed. They do not really constitute a menace to society, because they are so foolish, so stupid in their methods, and so readily captured, that their return to prison is inevitable. Their vanity is beyond belief. Nothing delights the habitual lag more than to have a photograph of his wife and children on his shelf, and these he displays with every evidence of pride to the few people who visit him in a humane spirit.

One has heard a great deal about the romance of crime, and I dare say in some respects the criminal is a romantic individual. But a great deal of the romance is sheer imagination, Men like Dick Turpin have been exalted by imaginative novelists into the character of something chivalrous and splendid. Dick Turpin was a butcher boy, a horse thief, and a coarse, illiterate boor. The glamour of his ride to York on "bonny Black Bess" is chiefly remarkable for the fact that he never did ride to York, but to Lincoln, where he engaged in horse thieving.

Crippen was a much more intriguing figure than any of those ancient "heroes" of crime,

Yet I will not deny that in my experience, even apart from the serious case of the Snake woman, I have been the witness of more than one incident which could, without any stretch of imagination, be described as romantic.

When I was in Gloucester Gaol, after my meeting with the snake woman, my first conviction, I met a man named Towner, a well, set-up, good-looking fellow of twenty-six; he had been arrested in Gloucester itself on a charge of defrauding the Post Office, and was serving a sentence of nine months' hard labour. He and I were together in the tailor's shop. I was serving six months for theft committed on the Cornish express, and our sentences expired together.

The romance really began with my steal. There was a lawyer who had come up from Plymouth to sell some properties. I got to know of this through a "nose" who made a profitable business by supplying information to criminals, and I followed him for three days before I stepped into the same carriage that was carrying him back to Plymouth. My objective was a black leather bag which he carried with him, and which he put beside him on the seat of the carriage.

His name, and of course I am giving a fictitious one, was Boglant, and he was a type of family lawyer—a sour, scowling, miserable-looking man—whom it was a real pleasure to rob.

At the end of the train was a carriage which was to be slipped at Swindon for Gloucester and Cheltenham, and my job was to get the bag in reasonable time before we reached Swindon, make my way to the Gloucester coach before it was disconnected, and escape as well as I could. With this object I had brought, inside a large brown kit-bag, an exact replica of the lawyer's black bag, and my job was to ring the changes.

I put my brown bag on the seat and strolled along the corridor on a tour of inspection. I had made a very careful study in preparation for this job, and what I was looking for was the electric wire which connects the dynamo beneath the carriage with the lighting apparatus, and the switch wire which runs the length of the train and has its termination in the guard's van. It is the business of the guard to turn on the lights before any long tunnel is reached, and I had chosen a tunnel to the west of Didcot for my purpose.

I had no difficulty In discovering the switch wire, and when we were about a quarter of an hour from the tunnel I took some wire-cutters from my pocket, cut the strand, and made my way carelessly back to the compartment, where the lawyer was sitting hunched up reading a newspaper.

I opened my own bag, pretending to study its contents, but in reality gripping the replica of the lawyer's bag which it contained, and no sooner had we plunged into the darkness of the tunnel than, slipping it out with one hand, and taking the lawyer's bag with the other, I made a quick exchange. It was not a long tunnel, and we soon again emerged to the light, where he found me sitting opposite to him. I saw him glance at the bag by his side, and a little frown gather on his face, and for a moment I thought he had detected the exchange. But no, he was apparently satisfied, which was a testimonial for me, for I had spent a very long time in making the dummy bag as exactly like his as it was possible.

"They ought to turn these lights on in the tunnels," he complained, and I warmly agreed.

Presently I asked:

"Does this train stop at Gloucester?"

And he looked over his paper.

"No," he said, "this is a through train to Plymouth. Exeter is the first stop. The Gloucester portion is in the rear; the carriages slip at Swindon."

In mock alarm, I gathered up my bag containing its precious contents, and hustled off into the rear of the train, and was only just in time, for the guard and an attendant had already detached the covered alleyway between the coaches. The carriage slowed at Swindon, and getting out on to the platform, I saw the other portion disappearing in the distance. A quarter of an hour later, having been attached to a local train, we pulled out, and I lost no time in making an examination of the bag contained in mine. It was locked, and I was glad to know that I had guessed its weight fairly accurately when I had loaded up the bag which I had passed to the lawyer with old books and papers.

Two slashes of my knife revealed its contents. To my dismay, there was no money, with the exception of about eighty pounds contained in an envelope, and marked punctiliously, as a lawyer would mark it, "Cash Sale No. 4, Motorcar."

He had been selling the effects of an estate which he was administering, and I presumed that No, 4 Motor car was part, of the property. The rest of its contents were bundles of documents, and I turned them disconsolately over, cursing my bad luck. I expected the old man to have taken all the proceeds of his sale in cash, and all I had got was a beggarly eighty pounds.

There was one thin envelope sealed and marked in pencil, "Fetter Lane Safe Deposit." In ink was written "Elsie Doran, will of Bertram Doran." What attracted my attention to this was the fact that it was half torn across. That struck me as strange, for the tear was a new one. The first thing I did was to take the bag and all its papers, and waiting until we crossed a stream, threw them through the open window into the water. The money I put, into my pocket, and as I did so I saw that I had omitted to throw out the "Elsie Doran" envelope.

Just at that moment the train began stopping at what I knew was a wayside station where we were not due to stop. Running into the corridor, I looked out of the window, and my heart for a moment sunk. There were three policemen in uniform standing on the platform. I dashed back to the carriage, took the envelope, and threw it out of the window, watching to see where it fell. The wind carried it down the steep embankment to a clump of bushes, and I had hardly seen its fate before the carriage door opened and an inspector of police came in.

"This is the man," he said.

To cut a long story short, the lawyer had discovered his loss almost as soon as the carriage was slipped, and had telegraphed information to the police. I was taken to a little village lock-up and searched, but beyond the money nothing was found upon me. I say beyond the money, but that was quite sufficient to secure my conviction, for Boglant had taken the numbers of the notes in his pocket-book.

I expected at least that I should be sent to the assizes, but to my delight I was dealt with summarily, and given six months' hard labour.

I shall never forget the lawyer's look of disgust when he heard sentence passed.

When I was in the cell awaiting my transfer to the gaol the gaoler brought the old man along, and we had an interview through the broad, square peep-hole.

"Now look here, Smith," he said, "I bear you no malice, but if you will tell me what you did with the papers you took out of my bag, I will give you ten pounds."

"I chucked them in the river," I said, "with the bag. They seemed a very uninteresting lot of documents."

"I dare say they did," he snarled. "Did you throw all of them into the river?"

"Every one," said I promptly.

As a matter of fact, I had forgotten the "Elsie Doran" envelope, or honestly I should have told him, for I had no particular reason for keeping back that information.

He asked me one or two further questions, and left. I might say, in passing, that in spite of the fact that I gave him all the information in my power, he conveniently forgot the ten pounds he had promised me.

This man I met in Gloucester Gaol was, as I say, a fairly decent fellow, with a good education and a considerable sense of decency. We agreed to meet in London after our releases, but, as a matter of fact, we were discharged on the same day, and travelled to London together.

He told me a great deal about the underworld which I never knew. There was a meeting place at Finsbury, a sort of Bohemian dance club which afforded people on the crook an opportunity of forgathering. I must confess that I was agreeably surprised when I saw the club, which occupied two floors. It was well conducted, nicely but not extravagantly furnished, and I was told that it was a model of what clubs should be. The men who ran and frequented the place could not afford to have any kind of scandal, and so it was more possible to get drink out of hours at any of the fashionable West-End clubs than at this thieves' kitchen.

Membership was not confined to one sex, and when I turned up to meet my friend I found him sitting at a little table taking tea with a pretty girl. I was surprised to find a girl of her appearance in such a resort. She was evidently a lady. You will judge of my surprise when Towner said:

"This is a friend of mine, Elsie; we came out of 'stir' together."

She looked at me with a cold, appraising glance, and nodded.

"If Gloucester is any worse than Holloway, I congratulate you," she said quietly.

"Holloway?" I said, startled. "You don't mean Holloway Prison? You haven't been there?"

She nodded and smiled, but it was one of those smiles which have no real humour in it, and I thought I detected a hint of pain and shame behind the brave show she made.

When we left the place Towner told me her history. She had come to London as a governess, and when she rejected the attentions of the father of the children whom she was teaching, a charge was faked against her, and she was sent to prison for three months on her first offence. Perhaps it is unfair to say that the charge was faked. A valuable diamond brooch had been found missing, and she was accused and arrested. I have every reason to believe that the woman who lost the brooch, the wife of this man who had persecuted her, found it, and rather than admit that she was in the wrong, and lay herself open to an action for false imprisonment, she secreted the brooch in the girl's room. At any rate, I am convinced that this was a genuine miscarriage of justice.

In prison she met other women, and after vainly attempting to secure work she drifted into a criminal gang.

"She hates the life," said Towner; "and I have done my best to keep her straight. If I could get a bit of money together, I would ask her to marry me, and take her to Canada."

"Why don't you marry her to start with?" said I.

He shook his head.

"Not as I am situated," he said seriously. "It wouldn't be fair—what chance would she have as the wife of a crook?"

"What was she in prison for last?" I asked curiously.

"For getting a situation with forged references," said Towner. "She wants to go straight, that I'll swear, but what can she do? And yet her father was a rich man. He left all his property to a cousin. Apparently he had a quarrel with her mother just after he made the will, and before the child was born. When he died this will was produced, and every penny has gone to a swine of a lawyer."

Suddenly I remembered.

"Elsie! What is her other name?" I

"Doran," he said; and I gasped.

"What was the lawyer's name?"

"A young fellow named Boglant."

"A young man?" I asked.

"Yes; his father is a lawyer, too. Old Boglant is one of the hardest nuts in Plymouth."

"Elsie Doran," I repeated; and then I told him the story of the lawyer's bag and the envelope I had found half torn across.

"Are you sure?" he asked quickly. "Did you say that it was the will of Bertram Doran?"

"That was written in pencil across the top, and it had been torn."

"It is the will that her father made after the other," said Towner excitedly. "She always felt there was one. We must see her at once."

He called a taxi and we drove to a quiet street in Holloway, where Elsie Doran occupied two rooms. She was surprised to see us, and no more surprised than the landlady, who had some doubt about admitting us, until I explained that I was Elsie Doran's lawyer, and must see her at once.

She listened in silence while we told the story.

"I am sure that is it," she said; "but what is the good?"   .

"I'm going to make a search of the railway embankment. I know the exact spot where the paper was thrown," said I.

"Six months ago?" She shook her head. "I don't think you will find it, Mr. Smith; and if you do, it will hardly have survived the rains and storms of the past six months."

"Four months and a half, to be exact," said I. "There is a chance, because the place I threw it was not part of the station premises, and the cleaners would not go to the trouble of tidying the bushes at the bottom of the embankment."

Towner and I left the next morning by train, and we reached the wayside station soon after one o'clock.

The station-master recognised me immediately, and greeted me with a broad grin. I told him that I had lost a pocket-book when I had been arrested, and was anxious to find it; and he was sympathetic, as all law-abiding people are sympathetic to criminals when they think that they are getting the better of the law. He was quite certain that I had thrown fabulous sums of money from the railway carriage window before I was arrested, and volunteered to help. I think he was surprised when I accepted the offer of his assistance.

We trudged along the embankment, and came at last to the spot where I had thrown the envelope. I explained to the station-master that it was a paper and not money, and he shook his head.

"I don't think you'll find it," he said; "we had a flood here two months ago. All those fields"—he pointed—"were under water, and the floods came half-way up the embankment."

Mentally I agreed with him, but we began to search, although I was certain that we were foredoomed to failure. The bushes were covered with verdure, and there was not a trace of any kind of paper to be seen; but, nevertheless, I did not lose heart, and in the middle of my search I remembered that I had located the exact spot where the envelope finally rested, because it stood in a direct line with a large elm tree in the middle of a near-by field.

We spent two hours in the search, and I was giving it up, when suddenly the station-master said:

"There's a paper up there," and pointed up to a tree which overshadowed the bushes.

We found the will wedged between two twigs, absolutely dry, and not so much as discoloured.

Afterwards the station-master recalled the fact that the night I was arrested there was a heavy wind storm, and probably the envelope had blown to its resting-place, the only spot where it could be sheltered from the torrential rains which had followed.

With trembling fingers, Towner opened the flap and took out the document, and, looking at him, I saw his face was white.

"This is it," he said; "made by her father three months before his death, and actually witnessed by Boglant!"

The will left most of his property to his daughter; there were a few legacies to servants, a hundred pounds to Boglant, and certain provisions as to the disposal of his estate. The sum involved was a considerable one, something like sixty thousand pounds.

We reached Plymouth that night, and found the office of Boglant & Boglant was closed. Hiring a taxi, we drove out to his big house on the Torquay road, and I went in to interview him, leaving Towner outside.

He recognised me instantly, but to the fat-faced young man who sat with him at dinner I was, of course, a perfect stranger.

"Well, you scoundrel," said Boglant, "what do you want? If I had known you were 'Mr. Smith' I would have had you kicked out."

"Smith!" said young Boglant apoplectically. "Is this the blackguard that stole your bag, father?"

"I am the blackguard," said I gently.

"What do you want?"

"I want the name of a good lawyer to represent Elsie Doran," said I, "and probably you can recommend me one, as you know them all in these parts."

The old man's face went grey.

"What do you mean?" he said.

"I mean that amongst the documents that were not destroyed was the will of the late Bertram Doran, which left the whole of his property to his daughter, and which you kept, carefully stowed away in the Fetter Lane Safe Deposit, until you decided to draw it out and destroy it. You began by tearing it, and then decided that you would wait until you got back to Plymouth and burn it, that, being a safer method."

He collapsed into his chair.

"There is no other will," he said hollowly.

"There is another will which you have witnessed," said I gently.

"I suppose you have come to blackmail me," he growled, after a pause.

"If you gave me the wealth of the Indies that will would have to be proved," said I. "You are going to restore every penny you stole from this girl, and you will give me a thousand pounds for keeping my mouth shut. Otherwise, you and I will be meeting in B. Ward."

I can only add that he made restitution, and that he paid me my thousand. It is the only money I have ever made by blackmail, and it was very sweet to spend.

IV

THE MASTER CRIMINAL

Is there a real master criminal? I doubt it. John Flay was the nearest I have ever met, and it is strange that even in Dartmoor I had never met him, though I helped flog one of his agents and incidentally heard the first mention of his name.

I had not been in Dartmoor long before I was removed to the punishment cells, not as a victim, but as an official, if an orderly can be called an official. Until the second year of my confinement the punishment prisoners were merely insolent or lazy convicts, and in consequence were introduced to the plank bed and carpet slippers. On two occasions we had men who had run amok in the fields, who were brought into the punishment hall, struggling more like wild beasts than men, and thrown into the padded cell. One of these, however, was a genuine lunatic; the second was a brute who had tried to kill a warder, and for him there could be only one punishment. Day after day he went before the Visiting Justices, and I learnt that he had been sentenced to fifteen lashes with the cat-o'-nine-tails. But the sentence had to go to the Home Office for confirmation. It was a fortnight later before my warder ordered me to get out the triangle.

One cell in the punishment hall is used as an irons store; the walls are covered with handcuffs and leg-irons, and in the centre of the cell stands a steel triangle, which, with the assistance of another convict, I got out and fastened to the floor. At eleven o'clock the next morning the prisoner was brought out, his hands manacled, and attached to a chain running from a pulley at the top of the triangle. His legs were fastened to two of the steel uprights, and a warder turned a wrench which drew his hands high above his head.

I had never seen a man flogged before, and it was a pretty ghastly experience. I subsequently confirmed, as I then suspected, that the real punishment of flogging is that moment of time before the fall of the whip. The cat-o'-nine-tails in itself consists of a handle about eighteen inches long, covered with blue felt; it is a tremendously thick handle, and wants a man with a very big hand to encompass it. Suspended from this are nine cords, the tip of each being bound about by yellow silk. The warder who administers the flogging stands at a distance from his victim, generally a little to the left, and extends the arm holding the cat until the hanging thongs are within about six inches of the man's left shoulder. The doctor says "One," and the flogger brings the whip round his head so that the lash follows roughly the figure eight before it falls. It is this horrible whistling sound which, to my mind, is the devilish part of the punishment.

In flogging you are not allowed to hit above or below the shoulder-blades, and an expert warder—I believe they receive five shillings for each flogging—will not deviate by so much as an inch from the line where the lash originally falls. Many people are under the impression that flogging eventually kills a man because the whip falls across his kidneys. That, however, is a great mistake. The whip is not allowed to fall below the line I indicate; if it does, the doctor will stop the flogging.

The prisoner took his punishment without a word, and when it was finished I placed a big piece of lint, which I held in preparation, across the shoulders, fastened it so that it could not slip off, and the man was taken back to his cell,

"John Flay ought to have had this!" was only comment; and that was the first and only time Flay's name was mentioned.

I had hitherto doubted the existence of the master criminal, for it seemed to me that the man fared best who "worked lonely."

I say, without boasting, that I probably made more money by illicit processes than any other criminal in the business. I have literally made thousands and spent thousands. If I had been one of those saving criminals one reads about, but never meets, I should probably be the wealthiest man that ever went in or out of a gaol. As it was, I was poor but happy, for life is very sweet to a philosophical convict.

I once got into contact with a doctor, a man of good birth, who had been engaging in some swindling practice into which I was dragged at the last moment. When the jury had retired and we were waiting in the room below, he told me that if he got a term of penal servitude he intended finishing everything with a dose of cyanide potassium which he carried loose in his waistcoat pocket, and which the warders had overlooked in their search. I knew it was pretty certain that he was going to get from three to five years, just as I was as certain that I should get off with about three months, because the part I had played was an insignificant one, and as we were tried at the Hereford Assizes, where my record was not known, I did not doubt that the judge would take a very merciful view of my offence.

Before we went up to the dock I took the chief warder aside.

"That fellow has a dose of cyanide of potassium in his pocket," I said, "and he is liable to commit suicide unless you take some steps to deal with him."

I told him where the poison was concealed, and, cursing me heartily, he was searched, and the drug taken away from him.

Ah I expected, he got three years, and, as I had hoped, my sentence was twelve months in the second division. We were placed in adjoining cells, and bitterly he cursed me for a traitor and a blackguard because I had betrayed him. I waited till his wrath had burnt itself out, and then I said:

"My friend, you have only one period of life to live, and it is stupid to curtail what may be a most enjoyable experience. You will be out of prison in two and a half years, with all the world to rove in, and all the opportunities for making good before you. It is better to be a living thief than a dead bishop."

He served the first part of his sentence in the name prison an myself, and before he was taken off to Dartmoor, or Portland—I am not sure which—he found an opportunity for thanking me.

Suicide in the consequence of a diseased vanity. The thought of what people are saying about him drives a weak man mad, and he prefers the oblivion of death to the consciousness of their disapproval. I have never had any sympathy with suicides. Suicide, to my mind, is the most objectionable form that conceit can take. Much more do I sympathise with the attitude of an old lag I met in Dartmoor who had shot a policeman and did not expect to be released from prison until he was sixty-four.

"I shall be in the prime of life," he said to me one day, when we were shovelling coke in the big yard, "and I am going to have a good time. I haven't decided whether I shall go to Brighton or Margate to live."

I was able to give him a tip as to how to get an honest living, and when I came out of gaol, by a curious coincidence, I came upon him, and saw that he had carried out my suggestion. He had a piano organ, on the front of which was painted, in legible letters, the words I had suggested, and which he had evidently committed to memory. They ran:

"I am an ex-convict, and have spent twenty-five years in prison. This is the only honest way of making a living which does not bore me stiff."

He told me he was taking between five and six pounds a day in silver and copper. The British public love frankness, and they have, thank Heaven, a sense of humour. He told me that the police never dared to move him on for fear of exciting the indignation of the populace, and that when they did shift him from any pitch, a perfect hail of silver coins came from his sympathetic audience.

It was more than an ordinary coincidence, this meeting with William Billington, for whilst I was talking to him there came upon the scene the most remarkable man I have met in my criminal career.

A great deal has been written about John Flay, arid I suppose he will go down to history as one of those legendary heroes of the underworld about whom romantic writers wax enthusiastic. In appearance he looked like one of those American professional men whom one meets at the holiday resorts on the Continent. A tall, clean-shaven man, with gold-rimmed spectacles and a broad brimmed black hat, he was always dressed neatly and unobtrusively, and not once during my knowledge of him did I ever see him wear an article of jewellery. He contented himself with a nickel watch that you can buy for five shillings, which was attached to a brown leather guard, and yet, in spite of his lack of ostentation, there was a time when John Flay was worth nearly half a million pounds.

Beyond the incident to which I have referred, I had never heard of him, which was remarkable, remembering that I had spoken to some of the best-known criminals in England, but it was evident, from the respectful manner in which old William greeted him, that he was a person of some importance. At first I thought he was the chief constable, and when he had gone, I asked William:

"Who is your classy friend?"

William looked uncomfortable.

"Oh, that's Mr. Flay," he said awkwardly; and I could get no other information out of him.

I saw Flay again that evening in the lounge of the hotel where I was staying. He came across to me. He was smoking a long and particularly fragrant cigar.

"So you're a book, are you?" he said, without any preamble. "William tells me that he met you in the Home of Rest. I am John Flay."

"I have never heard of you," I said coolly. "What is your particular line of authority—police or prisons?"

"Neither," he said, and offered me a cigar. "You're called Smith, and I suppose that is not your name. You were a gentleman, too."

"I am still," said I, biting off the end of the cigar, and lighting it.

He looked at me for a long time scrutinisingly, and then he said:

"The worst of you fellows is that you have no organisation at the back of you. You take all sorts of chances that you need not take, and at the critical moment, when you want a friend, he is not there to lend a helping hand. You'd be an invaluable man—in an organisation."

"What kind of organization?" I asked flippantly. "Are you a member of one of those gangs one reads about in the magazines?"

He took no notice of my jest, but continued to eye me keenly.

"You wouldn't take all the profit, but then you'd take some of it, and be sure of getting it without trouble." He leant across the table and lowered his voice. "Suppose you were at Boulogne next Monday week with a diplomatic passport, which means that your baggage wouldn't be searched, and somebody coming off the mail-train handed you a bag and you took it aboard, and brought it to an address I will give you in London, would that be worth two hundred?"

I returned his gaze now, for I knew that he was talking business.

"What will be in the bag?" I asked.

"That will be nothing to do with you! You could be, for the first time in your life, absolutely innocent. But I will put your mind at rest. There would be a million francs in the bag, and I am only offering you two hundred because about ten people have to get their share, and then the notes have to be changed. Would you like to do the job?"

I nodded.

"What about the diplomatic passport? That's rather a difficult one to get."

"Don't worry; the passport will be in your hands before you leave London. Maundy and Spear are the two detectives on duty on the boat. Do you know them?"

I shook my head.

"Do they know you? That's a little more important."

"No," I said. "I don't imagine so."

"I shouldn't have asked you," said Flay thoughtfully, "only the man whom I had intended to bring the bag across doesn't quite look the part. You can carry clothes, and you look rather like a young Foreign Office official."

I laughed.

"Aren't you afraid of my double crossing you?" I asked; and his saturnine features creased in a smile.

"No, I don't think so," he said quietly. "I never make mistakes in choosing my man."

Little more than a week later found me on the platform at Boulogne, and my presence was explained to the officials by the beautifully forged diplomatic passport which had brought me ashore. It lent likelihood to the proceedings that I was to meet the Orient express, and that the man from whom I had to take the bag was travelling in the Constantinople coach. There is nothing remarkable in the meeting of this train by diplomatic officials. In fact, I believe it is done twice or three times a week.

The train came in, and a stout, bearded Frenchman stepped lightly down and looked at me quickly.

"M'sieur Smith?" he said.

I nodded, and he placed in my hand a big leather portfolio. I took it from him, and, with a nod to the Customs officials, I passed through the office on to the wharf. I had already secured my embarkation ticket, and in a few minutes I was sitting at ease in the handsome little cabin of the Invicta.

At Folkestone I was again saved the bother of a Customs' examination, and the coupé which had been reserved for me on the Pullman was very inviting and warm after a somewhat rough crossing.

At Victoria a handsome motor-car was waiting for me; it had been pointed out to me before I left London, and I jumped in, to find it was already occupied by a man, who spoke no word until we were clear of the station.

"Here is your money," he said, and handed me two crisp notes.

"And here is your bag," I smiled. "It was an easy job. I'd live honestly if I had a commission like that every week."

He dropped me at the corner of Whitehall, and neither of us mentioned the name of Flay. I had hardly stepped upon the pavement, and the car moved off, before a hand touched me on the shoulder, and I turned to see the jovial face of Inspector Stelling, of Scotland Yard.

"Hallo, Smith!" he said. "Getting into society?"

"Yes," I replied.

"Nice car that," said Stelling, looking after the retreating limousine.

"Not a bad car. It belongs to a friend of mine who is trying to reform me," said I.

"Is John Flay trying to reform you?" said Stelling, in mock surprise. "Where have you come from?"

I was silent.

He evidently knew the car, and I wondered why so astute a man as John Flay should be identified with such a handsome machine. My wonder was set at rest by his next words.

"That's the car Flay uses," he said. "It is supposed to be the property of his doctor, who is as big a crook as he is. Where have you come from, Smith?"

"From Victoria Station," I said. "I have been down to Brighton."

"You came up on the Continental," he said very patiently. "I saw you and followed you here."

And then, looking past him, I saw that there was a car drawn up a dozen yards away from where I had been set down, and evidently he had followed us in this.

"Bless my life, Stelling," said I blandly, "we poor, innocent crooks can keep no secrets from you. Yes, I went down to meet a friend at Folkestone, but he didn't turn up."

"You had a bag when you came out of the Pullman—a sort of portfolio. Where is it now?" said Stelling. "And I am sure you will excuse my curiosity when I tell you that the National Bank of France has been robbed of ten million francs."

"Good effort!" I said. "But I am no bank robber, Stelling, and so far as having a bag, I can only assure you that your eyes have deceived you. I carried no bag or portfolio, or anything that would look like a bag or a portfolio. Oh, yes," I said, as though I had suddenly remembered. "I carried the bag of a lady when she was alighting from the Pullman, and gave it to her when she got into her taxi."

It was a shot at random, but I knew that the station platform was so crowded that he could not have been able to observe my every movement.

"I guess you're lying," he said. "But it doesn't matter very much. I know where to find you when I want you."

"May our meeting be long deferred," said I, and left him, feeling just a little uncomfortable.

I found means of getting into touch with John Flay that night. He had given me a telephone number where I could call him, and I told him briefly and guardedly what had happened.

"That's all right," he said. "I saw Stelling following us."

"Were you in the car?" I asked.

"I was driving," was the laconic reply. "Don't worry. Good-night!"

About a week after that I was working on a scheme I had invented, having as its object the removing of a petrol millionaire's superfluous cash. It was a very ingenious scheme, and it has been one of my regrets that I never carried it into execution. What really arrested me in my career was a meeting with Inspector Stelling at a certain bar near Piccadilly Circus. It was, I thought, an accidental meeting, but the truth was, as I learnt, that he had had me under observation for a week, and this fact alone was sufficient to postpone my great attack upon the oil-King.

"I am going to tell it to you straight, Smith, for I feel that I can trust you," he said. "I want Flay very badly, and if you can give me any kind of help to rope him in, you will not regret it."

I told him then and there, and with perfect sincerity, that I knew nothing more about Flay than that I had done one job for him.

"I won't ask you to tell me what the job was," he said shortly, "because I know. You were the man who brought across the stolen notes from Boulogne. They were handed to you by a man named Lefèvre, who was arrested the next day. I am not going to go into the matter at all. Flay may have been the organiser—he certainly was the receiver; but it is the business of the French police to track him down if they can." Then he told me what I had half suspected, namely, that John Flay was the genius who organised more clever burglaries than any other man in England. He not only organised them, but he financed burglars who wanted a kit, he paid for their defences when they were arrested, and generally acted as a service bureau to the underworld. In return, he got the lion's share of most of the crimes. He handled the jewellery and the stolen stuff, and marketed them in some mysterious way which the inspector had not been able to discover.

Flay I did not see again for nearly three months. I had no need of him, and apparently he had no particular use for me. I was down to my last sovereign when I got information about a house at Highgate which was reputedly kept by an aged miser, Mr. Wellinghall. My informant got his information from an old woman who acted as a sort of daily housekeeper. She had never seen her employer; he was eccentric and apparently a little mad, and had all his food sent up to him on a little hand-lift from the kitchen, and never under any circumstances appeared in public. He dusted and swept his own room, and was apparently a man of wealth and substance, for he always paid in cash, and nobody had ever seen a cheque of his. That meant he had a lot of money on the premises, and since I have a rooted objection to people who hoard their fortune, I determined to give Mr. Wellinghall a look up.

It was a big, rambling house, neglected and dirty in appearance, but an easy house to burgle, I should think. The night I chose for my preliminary visit I was again checked by Stelling, who overtook me as I was walking across the path.

"Have you seen Flay lately?"

"No," I replied.

"Now, come across. Smith," he began coaxingly. "You know he was in that picture steal."

I remembered having read in the morning that somebody had taken two pictures from one of the Midland art galleries, and that they were worth some twenty thousand pounds, but beyond noting the fact and wondering in what manner these huge pictures could have been taken away without attracting the notice of the police, I had not given the matter much thought.

"I know you weren't in it," Stelling went on, "because my people have been watching you; but Flay is in it. I swear."

"I ask you to believe me, Stelling," I said, "that, as a lover of art, I strongly disapprove of picture stealing. I know nothing more about Flay than what I have already told you, and that if I did know, I should not squeal. Happily, I don't."

This seemed to satisfy Stelling. We had a drink together, and we parted.

I waited until it was dark before I went to Highgate on my second visit, and arriving there, I made a thorough reconnaissance of the house.

The house stood in a rank garden, and the back window, which I forced, gave me no trouble at all. I found myself in an empty room, littered with packing-cases and pieces of old furniture and the like, and made my way carefully into the passage and up the stairs.

At last I came to the small room which had been described to me, and which I knew lay next to the secret apartments of the miser. I carried no weapon, but a jemmy and the usual tools, in the use of which I had become almost an expert. The door was locked. No gleam of light showed under, and with the utmost care I inserted my skeleton key, and, after three attempts, succeeded in turning the lock. The room, as I expected, was in darkness. There was light in another room leading from this, which, when I put my lamp over it, proved to be a dilapidated drawing-room.

Stealthily I moved across the carpeted floor toward the light, and my hand was on the knob, when there was a blinding flash of light. All the lamps in the drawing-room had been suddenly put on; I heard the click of the switch, and I spun round to meet the level barrel of a revolver. But it was not the pistol, and it was not the sight of the two big canvases propped against the wall at one end of the room, that took my breath away. It was the unexpected apparition of Mr. Flay. He was as astonished as I.

Suddenly he put down the pistol, and laughed silently.

"Well, I'm hanged!" he said. "What are you doing here?"

Without waiting for me to reply, he went on:

"I suppose you've heard of the old miser who lived in this house. Well, my boy, I am the old miser who sleeps all day and mustn't be disturbed on any account."

"I haven't heard that story," said I. "I hope you will accept my apologies, Mr. Flay, for intruding upon your privacy."

He was still laughing silently to himself. "We must get a bottle of wine on this; it is the funniest thing that has happened to me for years," he said. "Yes, this is my Aladdin's cave, and you are the only man who knows of its existence."

He went to his bin, a black, square box near the fireplace, and took out a gold-topped bottle, opened it deftly, and filled two glasses which he took from the cupboard.

"Here's better luck in your next enterprise," he said; and at that moment the door opened, and in walked Stelling.

And behind Stelling I could see the stairway was crowded with "splits."

"It's a cop," said Flay philosophically. "This gentleman is not in this," he said, pointing to me. "He's a visitor."

"I dare say," said Stelling sarcastically, "and now he is going on a visit to Portland."

They gave John Flay seven years, and to me they gave twelve months, and I was innocent of everything—except burglary!

V

THE HOUSE OF DOOM

I should very much like to meet the man who said, "Never interfere between husband and wife," and take him by the hand. He is probably dead.

One of the first things I did when I came out of prison was to look round for a nice genteel way of swindling the public. Perhaps it is not exactly right to say I looked round when I came out. I had been looking round mentally all the time I had been in prison, and I hit upon an ideal plan, which I proceeded to put into execution.

In prison I met a man named Manson, who was doing time for frauds on bookmakers, and he gave me an idea that enabled me to live twelve months without breaking the law. I might say that my intention was to give the law as bad a jolt as possible, but, as things turned out, it was not necessary. On my release from prison I met a friend who was a member of a well-known smart night club, and he took me to lunch there.

It was the day before the Derby was run, and the club had a sweepstake, in which he took ten tickets, one of which he gave to me for luck. By the oddest chance I drew the winner, and received the magnificent sum of £450. I had now sufficient capital to carry out the scheme I had formed in prison.

I took a furnished flat in Jermyn Street, and securing a directory from a Turf society, I personally wrote to three hundred bookmakers throughout the kingdom, giving them the name of my bank, and requesting that a credit account be opened. It was a long and tedious business; it took me three days to write the letters. Of the three hundred, two hundred wrote back, telling me that an account had been opened in my favour, giving me a credit limit from £10 to £50. I started betting on the Monday and, nearly every bet I made cost me £3 for telegraph fees alone. My intention was to take a race, which had about eight runners and, reducing the eight to about four that had any chance, to telegraph fifty bookmakers one horse, another fifty the second horse, and so on. In this way I should be certain to find the winner, and I need not bother with the losers.

At the end of the week, when the cheques and the bills came in, I should have a sure profit, and the men who had won could whistle for their money,

But on the very first day an extraordinary thing happened. The butler, who I also think was the proprietor of the block of flats in which I was staying, told me that he had a tip for the four o'clock race from his nephew, who was head lad In one of the Wiltshire training stables, and I departed from my original plan and wired this horse to two hundred and seven bookmakers. It won at eight to one, and as the least I had had on was £2, the profit on my day's working was an enormous one. It gave me, in fact, nearly seven thousand pounds profit, and eliminated the necessity for running crook,

On the Thursday, thinking that I might have some difficulty with the bookmakers if I had only backed one horse, and that a winner, I decided to send them all a horse which I had picked out for no particular reason, except that none of the newspapers had picked it, and therefore it was likely to lose. To my amazement, it won at a hundred to eight.

My week's betting—I backed two losers on Friday—produced me a profit of ten thousand, three hundred pounds. There was really no reason in the world why I should ever steal again, I have always contended that we people of good birth are the only people who have acquired the art of spending money; but, encouraged by my success, I prepared to operate the bookmaker robbing plan on a more elaborate scale.

There was a small printing business in a South Eastern suburb for sale, and for a few hundreds I purchased it, leaving its conduct to an old man who had been in the employ of the firm for years. I chose this particular business because it had rather a high-sounding name. There had been three partners— Witherby, Dixshalt and Green. At the cost of another hundred pounds, I turned this office into a limited liability company, took an office in the city, and furnished it. "Witherby, Dixshalt and Green, Ltd.," looked good upon acetate notepaper, so did my name as managing director, the list of my agents in Cape Town, Sydney, New York, Bombay and Calcutta, and a further list in which I described the firm as printers and publishers, stationers, printers' agents, etc.

For the first time in my career I used my own name, but this time I tackled one of the London bookmakers, and asked for credit on a more extensive scale. Unfortunately, I also wrote to a big paper maker, in my capacity as managing director, and ordered an immense quantity of paper, purposely putting the figure per pound much lower than the market price, which I had taken the trouble to ascertain. I did this with the intention of establishing my stability, believing the firm would write back, regretting that they could not fulfil the order at the price. Unfortunately, the particular paper I had asked for—and I had chosen the quality and character at random—had been overstocked in their warehouse, and, to my horror, they confirmed the order and informed me that supplies would be made the following week. They also enclosed an invoice for eighteen hundred pounds. I thought I would be able to get out of this by writing cancelling the order. I was too interested in the re-opening of my betting career to bother about paper.

I am not exaggerating when I say that at the end of the week I was over thirty thousand pounds in credit; but before these bills could be paid, I was arrested on the charge of running a dud firm, my record was brought up against me, and I was also identified as the associate of a man who had committed a number of frauds upon bookmakers.

I found that the paper makers had put through an enquiry as to my stability long before I had cancelled the order, and had placed the matter in the hands of the police, when they discovered that my highly sounding company was only a tiny little printing office.

Anyway, the "busy fellows" were after me like a pack of hounds, and I was sent down for ten years—a very serious sentence. And I might have been back at this moment in Dartmoor, but for the fact that a flaw was discovered in the indictment, and, before the Court of Criminal Appeal, my conviction was quashed.

My first step on my release was to claim the money the bookmakers owed me. They could produce no proof that I intended defrauding them, and on the threat of taking the matter before Tattersall's Committee, I managed to collect a very considerable sum of money, the major portion of which was now in my possession. And I left England for Wiesbaden in double quick time.

From Wiesbaden I went on to Marienbad, and it was whilst I was in Marienbad that I met Kiltin and his wife. The man was a swindler of some kind; I have never been quite certain what his game was, but he had made a large sum of money and was engaged in "doing it in." A hopeless vulgarian, a man whose brutal and foul tongue knew no restraint when he was angered, he had the strength of an ox and no little skill as a fighter.

I believe he had originally ornamented an East End boxing ring, and had graduated to crime by those methods with which the public is so familiar.

His wife was a slim, pretty girl, socially his superior, I should imagine, passionately devoted to this great brute, and in some terror of him.

The man, however, had passed his boxing days, was undertrained and overfed, but still a dangerous animal to tackle, and I should never have dreamt of touching him, but for the fact that my bedroom was next to Kiltin's, and I was awakened at three o'clock in the morning by the sound of a woman's sobs, and the unmistakable noise of blows being administered by a heavy hand.

In Germany it is not unusual for men to beat their wives, but it is a practice to which I have never grown accustomed, and I was out of bed and in the passage knocking at their door before I realised what I was doing. The man opened the door and scowled at me.

"What do you want?" he asked.

I had met him the previous day, and he recognised me.

"Is anything wrong?" I demanded; and then I saw over his shoulder the huddled figure on the floor; her cheek was blood-stained, he had cut her mouth with his huge fist, and one of her eyes was red and swollen.

Kiltin had been drinking, I think, and I afterwards learned that this was the second time there had been such an occurrence, and that he had been threatened with expulsion from the hotel by the management If it happened again.

"You don't mean you have been hitting that girl, do you?" I asked.

His answer was a blow aimed wildly at me, which, if it had reached home, would have done me no good at all. But now I was as fit as possible. Penal servitude is a fine training for a man with a taste for athletics, and I dodged the blow and landed him two on the point before he realised what was happening. And then the woman, struggling to her feet, came at me like a fury. She scratched and bit and screamed, and before I knew what had happened, the corridor was full of people. I was glad to get back to my room.

In the morning the Kiltins received notice to go, and their luggage was brought down to the hall as soon as it was packed. I saw the man and he saw me. Coming over to where I sat, he glowered down at me, his hands in his pockets.

"The first time I ever meet you, my friend, I'll fix you," he said.

"It will be a pleasant change alter wife-beating," sad I. "You used to be in the Ring, I'm told—you should make a champion."

He was apoplectic with rage, and I was prepared for him to hit at me there and then, but apparently he thought better of it, and left me, muttering under his breath.

When I got back to London, I put through a few inquiries, and discovered, as I had thought, that the man was a known bad character. He had been in prison four or five times, mostly for offences against the person, assault, unlawful wounding, etc. Consideration for safety induced me to move West. I took a little house at Torquay, and had quite a pleasant time living on my ill-gotten gains.

Unhappily for me, the Kiltins came to Torquay, too, and, by an odd coincidence, took a furnished house in the same road as I was living. I met Mrs. Kiltin on the beach road, and she scowled at me as though I were her worst enemy instead of being, as I had intended, her best friend.

There was living in Torquay at the time a Colonel Mansil, who had a wonderful collection of emeralds. Some infernal person told me about this collection, and naturally my mind was occupied with the colonel and his property when it should have been engaged in securing a lead to a better life,

The long and short of it was that I broke into the colonel's handsome house in Babbacombe, or, rather, St. Mary Church, was returning at four o'clock in the morning with about two hundred pounds' worth of stones in my pocket—the bulk of the collection was in a safe—when, passing the Kiltins' house, which I had to, I saw Mrs. Kiltin standing on the doorstep in her nightgown, and bearing the marks of a recent thrashing.

I hesitated. What could I do? Any interference on my part must inevitably have the effect of making her hate me worse than she did. And yet my heart bled to see that frail figure standing on a chilly morning shivering before the closed door of her house.

"Can I be of any assistance?" I asked.

She turned her bruised face to me.

"Go away," she said hoarsely—"go away, or he will kill you, too."

She was so vehement that I hesitated no longer, and went on my way to my house.

I was arrested that afternoon. On whose information? On the information of Mrs. Kiltin, who had seen me returning, and had learnt that I had suffered a term of penal servitude for a similar offence. It was she, who, when she was reconciled to her husband that morning, and when she had heard that a burglar had broken in and stolen the emeralds, had gone straight to the police and told them all she knew.

As I say, never come between husband and wife.

I served my imprisonment in Exeter Gaol—I got the surprisingly light sentence of nine months' hard— and I carried with me to my confinement the memory of that brutal face of Kiltin, and the eager, venomous eyes of his wife as they sat side by side in the court and heard the evidence.

I hadn't been in gaol a month before Kiltin had the audacity to apply, on some pretext or another, for permission to see over the gaol, and secured a Home Office order, What excuse he gave, heaven knows, because the Home Office is very chary of granting these permissions, but there he was, strutting beside the chief warder, when I came out of my cell one afternoon to do a little window-cleaning on behalf of the State. His grin of triumph, however, produced no emotion in my placid bosom. I am impervious to scorn, and men of Kiltin's calibre are quite incapable of annoying me.

The warder was opening a cell door in order to show him what they looked like, and I had to pass him. As I got abreast of him he said, under his breath:

"Nice place this, eh?"

"You'll see it for yourself one of these days," I said in the same tone; but little did I dream that my prophecy would come true.

About four months later, when I was within a few weeks of release, I learnt that the condemned cell was occupied by a man who had been convicted of wife murder. His name I was not told. As a matter of fact, I had few opportunities for gossiping, for I held a responsible position—I was assisting the schoolmaster to bring order into the chaotic minds of the criminal Yokels of Devonshire.

A pending execution makes very little difference to the routine of the prison; you might imagine that there was nobody within those high red walls to whom every minute passed all too rapidly. The day before the execution I and the other privileged prisoner were marched out into the yard, through the little glasshouse where our photographs had been taken when we arrived, to the coach-house, which was about a dozen paces away. It is an ugly, rectangular little building, with a roof like an inverted V, and built into a tiny hillock; it is the dampest place in the prison. The prison van rests on two wooden runners which are laid across an open pit. We had to draw out the van and tidy up. The brick-lined pit is about eight feet deep, and I found that the two traps do not fall away directly from the entrance of the pit, but work on a fulcrum bar principle—I think that is the right term.

I noticed that there was an inch of water at the bottom of the pit, and then recalled the fact that it was in this little shed that Lee, of Babbacombe, suffered his great ordeal. It will be remembered that the trap would not fall, and the reason is apparent even to-day. The shed is so damp that, given a heavy fall of rain, such as had occurred the night before his execution, the wet trap would swell, and whilst it was true that they sawed away a portion of the trap, it was equally true that, in their agitation, the warders sawed at the wrong place! The walls, even when I saw them, were running with water, and the little lever at the left of the trap as you enter the shed, was thick with rust.

Set into the trap are two rings, and on one of the flaps I noticed a chalk mark like a letter "T". It was very faint, and I asked the warder, who was a genial sort of soul, what it meant. He then explained the procedure of execution. When a man is to be executed, the governor of the gaol notifies Pentonville, which is the headquarters of the prison system, and Pentonville sends down a rope, a linen "cap"— which is a small piece of coarse linen with elastic loops to go over the ears—and a piece of chalk, the chalk being intended to mark the place where the condemned man's feet will stand.

We cleared all the gear, cleaned the lever, and pulled up the trap which the warder tested. Brr! I shall never forget the thud and clang of that falling platform. In one corner of the shed is a further trap-door leading to a flight of stone stairs into the pit. It is down these stairs that the doctor passes to examine the body after the drop has fallen.

There was no sign of a rope, of course, but from wall to wall ran two beams, between which were three stout steel rods to which the rope is affixed.

I confess that I slept very well that night. I am told that prisoners are restless on the eve of an execution, but that did not apply to me. The man had committed a brutal murder, and I am a strong believer in the death penalty even for people who do not commit murders. For example, I think if the Government had any intelligence they would have hanged me, for I was a more dangerous criminal than any of the poor fools who fill the cells of Britain's prisons.

The night before, the prisoners who were in cells on that side of the ward which overlooked the execution-shed were moved to the opposite side, and we were kept locked in till five minutes past eight the next morning, I heard the bell toll, and in my imagination I heard the thunder of the falling trap, but it did not thrill me. Wilde, when he was in Reading gaol, suffered agonies in that moment and imagined more than the truth.

"The hangman with his gardener gloves,
Slips through the padded door,
And binds one with three leathern thongs,
That the throat may thirst no more."

At nine o'clock I and a man named Thayle were marched up to the shed. The door was locked and the chief warder was waiting outside. He unlocked the door and we went in, and I had my first glimpse of a judicial death.

When the cloth that hid the man's features was removed, I looked down upon the face of Kiltin!

THE LAST CRIME

The last time I came out of prison with the deputy's words ringing in my ears, "I think you are the worst man in the world," was a remarkable day for me.

I can't say that I was very much impressed by the deputy's moral sayings. Advice and admonition are more or less superfluous to a man of intelligence, who knows when he is doing wrong, who knows what must be the inevitable end if he continues in his wrong-doing, and who certainly has no need of another's point of view to urge him to the obvious course.

As I told the gentleman who wished to commit suicide, life is very sweet, and life does not necessarily mean freedom. It means the enjoyment of one's faculties. And they can be as well enjoyed by a philosopher in gaol as they can in a Hyde Park Lane Flat.

Throughout my career of crime I had been under the mistaken impression that my real identity was unknown to my aristocratic friends and relations. I never dreamt that my brother-in-law, so respectable a man, should advertise the fact that he was related to a felon. Nor did I dream that my dear sister, that cold, heartless, and ambitious woman, would make the delinquencies of her brother a subject for tea-table conversation.

And yet that is precisely what had happened I found.

On the evening of my day of release I went to a theatre. I recovered my clothes from the place where I had stored them, and transferred some of the money I had on deposit at my bank, and it was a considerable sum, to my current account.

I dined well and wisely, and strolled across to the Hay market to see a certain play which I had heard about from an artistic-minded convict. Nobody, of course, knew me, and to the average member of the audience, I had the appearance of a youngish middle-aged man who had probably been abroad. My face was tanned with the glorious sun of Devon, I was fighting fit and in the best condition, and as nature has endowed me with my share of good looks, I flatter myself that I put up a presentable appearance.

After the show was over I got my coat from the cloak-room and strolled into the vestibule, intending to walk to my hotel. Suddenly I heard a sweet voice say:

"Excuse me!" and I turned to meet a glorious pair of blue eyes and one of the prettiest faces it has been my lot to look upon. "How do you do, Captain Penman?" (I have camouflaged my name, naturally.)

Nobody had called me "Penman" for years, and I could not for the life of me place her, although her face was familiar.

"You don't know me, although we've met."

A smile trembled at the corner of her beautiful mouth, as though she were quietly amused.

"I am afraid I am very rude indeed, for I do not recall you," said I. "The fact is, I have been abroad."

She shook her head at me.

"Captain Penman, that isn't true," she said, lowering her voice. "Will you see me home?"

Nothing pleased me better, and I called a cab arid followed her into it.

She lived in St. John Street, Adelphi, and had a comfortable flat with two eminently respectable servants, who were waiting up for her when she arrived.

"I am going to have coffee, will you take a cup with me?" she asked. "And please take off your coat, Captain Penman."

She slipped her cloak from her dazzling white shoulders, and again looked at me quizzically.

"I know you are terribly puzzled as to where we met," she said. "The truth is that our first meeting was more unconventional than our second. I was in bed when I saw you last."

"In bed?" I gasped.

She nodded, still smiling.

"I think it was your first crime, Captain Penman, although perhaps your brother-in-law will not agree with me. And you escaped over the roofs of the houses in Portman Square, and you came into a room occupied—"

"Good lord, I remember!" I said. "You were the lady whose sleep I so brutally interrupted?"

She nodded.

My mind went back all those years, and I tried to recall the face that I had seen on that night. I remembered it was beautiful, but somehow I could not recall a definite vision.

"You are probably wondering why I am not in Portman Square now," she said quietly, "My father died penniless, but fortunately I had had a training at an art school, and I wrote a little. I am now a magazine illustrator. Yes, your brother-in-law told us all about it," she went on, after the coffee had come in and the servants had disappeared. "And your sister made no secret of the fact that she had been burgled by a man who held the Distinguished Service Order. What have you been doing? You have been in prison, I know."

"Several times," I admitted. "In fact, I am now one of the consistently regular patrons of Princetown's principal hotel."

She looked at me steadily, gravely, but not disapprovingly, I was glad to note.

"I have wanted to meet you for a long time," she said. "And once, when I was on a sketching tour across Dartmoor, I stayed for two whole days in Princetown, hoping to see you marched out with the other men."

"You should have called in and seen me at home," said I; and she laughed at my irony.

"What are you going to do now?" she asked.

"I haven't quite decided upon the type of crime, but it will be something exhilarating, you may be sure," I said.

"Do you like it—this life?" she asked, and I shrugged.

"Of course you don't like it, but I mean it isn't altogether abominable to you?"

"Not at all," said I. "It is very amusing in many ways. In some ways it is a bore."

"Did you ever meet in your travels a man named Price Wold?"

I shook my head.

"Is he one of us?" I asked, and a half smile came and faded upon her lips.

"He is not a convicted scoundrel," she said, and apologised hurriedly. "I mean he is a scoundrel but he has never been convicted. I wondered if you had ever heard of him. He was a soldier years ago. I am going to marry him," she added simply.

I could only stare at her.

"Marry an 'unconvicted scoundrel'?" said I. "You are taking rather a risk, aren't you?"

She nodded.

"Mother doesn't like it. She lives in the country with my aunt, and, poor soul, she doesn't know the reason I am getting married is to save her dear feelings. I don't know why I am telling you all this," she said with a nervous little laugh. "It was sheer caprice that made me approach you. I was hoping you were feeling a little sad yourself so that we could commiserate with one another."

"Why are you marrying this man?" I asked quietly. It seemed almost, as if f had known her for twenty years, we had fallen so quickly into the confidential strain.

"Because I must," she said. "Captain Penman, I suppose you are so well acquainted with the follies of the world that you won't be very shocked if I tell you that I had a love affair with my music master. In a sense it was quite innocent, though it might not have been but for the fact that my father found out in time. I had written him a number of letters; he was not a gentleman in the best sense of the word, though he was very fascinating to me.

"When I look back on that time I wonder if it was me at all," she said thoughtfully. "The letters I wrote to him were—well, they were foolish, I never think of them without shuddering. I was only a child at the time, and in many ways an ignorant child. I learnt afterwards, when the affair was broken off, that the man had boasted of our close acquaintanceship. As a matter of fact, it was through his indiscretion that my father got to know, I was terribly cut up at the time, but I thought the whole thing was over and done with and the memory of Carlo had passed from my mind, when I learnt, about three years ago, that the letters were in the possession of Price Wold, whom I had met at my father's dinners, and whom I had regarded as a very amiable middle-aged man, rather fat and talkative."

"I see," I said slowly, "Then your marriage is the price of the letters?"

She nodded,

"It sounds like a chapter from a 'shocker,' doesn't it?" she said unsmilingly. "But that is the truth. He has told me in so many words that unless I consent to marry him he is going to make my mother acquainted with the contents of the letters. That would kill her. She is so sensitive to scandal that my father never told her a word about the affair."

"Do you like him?" I asked.

"Who, Price Wold? I loathe him, I hate him!"

Her voice was vibrant with suppressed passion.

"I don't mind his being so much older than I, but there is something repulsive about the man. And he is a criminal, Captain Penman, a real criminal, greater than any you have met in your travels. I am perfectly sure that he has been living on blackmail for years. When I saw you in the vestibule, I wondered for a second if you knew him or if you had any influence with him. I know that you are quite famous amongst the people of the underworld. Ah! You did not like to hear that. It is the first time you have shown any sign of discomfort!"

"I am not exactly proud of being a little hero amongst the crooks of London," said I with some asperity, of which I was rather ashamed afterwards. "No, I do not know Mr. Wold, but if it will serve you in any way I will get acquainted with him. Where does he live?"

"At Babbington Chambers," she said, but shook her head again. "I don't think it would serve any useful purpose—meeting him, I mean. But it has been a great relief," she smiled, "to lay my burden on you and to pour my woes into a sympathetic ear. You are really not going to commit any further crimes, are you, Captain Penman?" she asked earnestly. "I shall hate it, knowing you. I am sure I couldn't sleep if I thought of you, now that I have met you, lying in a cell at Dartmoor or working with those horrid men in the fields."

I was silent. She had introduced into my life a novel embarrassment.

"Let us hope for the best," I said piously.

"But there is no sense in my hoping unless you are hoping, too," she said, "and now I am going to turn you out, for I have to get up at half-past five in the morning to finish a sketch. I always work best in early morning."

I had said good-bye to her, when I saw a long cord coiled upon the window ledge. I should not have spoken about it, but she followed the direction of my eyes.

"That is my milk cord," she said, "and it is appropriate that you should see it, after I have been boasting of my early hours. The milkman comes at six o'clock, whistles, and I let down the cord. It saves me a journey downstairs at an hour when I am not usually fully clad."

I don't know whether it was the cord, and the train of thought which that set in motion, or whether I had already begun to think things out subconsciously, but I left Beryl Manton with my plan of operation almost complete. The clock of St. Clement's Dane was chiming midnight when I came into the Strand, and, calling a taxi, I told him to drive me to the end of Knightsbridge, where Babbington Chambers was situated. I did not know, and had never heard of Wold, but I knew Babbington Chambers, an abiding place of the vulgarly rich and perhaps the most expensive flats in London.

The only man on duty at this time of night was the lift attendant, and as the lift was going up when I entered the swing doors, it was all to the good. Fortunately for me, my plan for getting upstairs unobserved failed, for the lift was an open one, and the attendant, an old soldier, checked its ascent.

"Are you looking for any number, sir?"

"Yes, I want Mr. Wold," I said.

I should eventually have had to go to the attendant and ask him, for I found that only one or two flats had name plates.

"His is number sixteen on the third floor. I'll take you up, sir."

"Thank you," I said.

"He's got a party to-night," said the attendant as the lift shot up. "I suppose you're going to it, sir?"

"That is my intention," said I.

I pressed the bell of No. 16, and a manservant opened the door. He seemed to take it for granted that I was one of the expected guests, for he took off my coat and hung up my hat.

"What name shall I give?"

"Captain Penman," said I, using my own name for the first time for many years.

The drawing-room into which I was shown was crowded with people. They were mostly girls of the chorus-girl type and the kind of young man one meets at night clubs, and everybody seemed more or less—well, I will say jovial. I hesitate to describe any woman as being under the influence of drink.

I knew my man the moment my eyes lit upon him. He was broad and gross of build, tall, red-faced, and black-haired, and he came towards me with a look of doubt on his face.

"How do you do, Wold?" I said. "You don't remember me? I am Eric Penman."

"Glad to meet you," he said; "but I don't quite place you."

"You invited me to come to your party a week ago," said I.

I thought it was likely that a man of that kind might, in his cups, issue invitations indiscriminately.

"Oh, did I?" he said, relieved. "I suppose when I met you at the Porters. I was so well bottled that night that I don't know whether I invited people or not."

With this he waved a general introduction to the company, and I became engulfed in a crowd of bright-eyed girls and half-drunken men, who were all trying to talk at once. In a second my arm was grabbed by a girl with bobbed hair and a heavily made-up face.

"Do you know Saucy?"

"Saucy?" said I, thinking she was referring to some girl who was present.

"Saucy Wold," she said. "Of course you know him!" with a little hiccough. "This is his last bachelor party; he is going to be married, he has just told us."

I will not attempt to describe the three hours of discomfort I spent in the heated atmosphere of Price Wold's drawing-room. Long before the company made a move, I slipped out of the room, watching a favourable opportunity when the servant had gone to his pantry to find more champagne, and, making my way along the heavy piled carpet of the corridor, I came at last to what I decided must be his bedroom. I shut the door and put on the lights, making a rapid search. In one corner of the room stood an old-fashioned secretaire. I pulled down the flap and opened the drawers, not daring to hope that Beryl's letters would be left so exposed.

The only thing I found was a loaded revolver, which I slipped into my pocket.

I began to search for secret drawers, but without success. And then I made a careful examination of the walls for some secret hiding-place, and found it behind an engraving—a small circular combination safe let into the wall. To attempt to open this without the code word was a waste of time. What I did find in one of the drawers was a dozen pairs of Indies' black silk stockings. This, in a way, was an unexpected windfall, for a silk stocking was the very thing I wanted. I did not stop to consider what those stockings were doing in a bachelor's bureau, but I had my own theory.

With a pair of nail scissors I found in the dressing-room I snipped the stockings in two and cut two eye-holes. This done, I fitted the broad end of the stockings over my head—it made an excellent mask. Then I looked about for a place of concealment, and found it in a long clothes cupboard at the further end of the room. All being ready, I switched out the lights, slipped off the mask, and returned to the hall, and, finding my hat and coat, removed it to the cupboard in Wold's room. Then I took up my stand in the cupboard and waited.

The dawn was breaking when Wold came into the room. I heard the mumble of his voice as he gave some instructions to his servant, and then the snick of the key as he locked the door.

I had a very considerable while to wait, for he took his time about disrobing. At last I heard the click of the lights going out, and the creak of his heavy body on the bed.

I had previously got into my black evening overcoat, and now, pulling the mask over my face and settling my top-hat upon my head, I opened the door gently and stepped out into the darkened room. There was no sound save his heavy breathing, and I listened at the door to discover if the manservant was still about. Apparently he had gone to bed, too.

When I had assured myself of this, I turned on all the lights, and Wold sat up in bed, his mouth wide open, glaring at the strange figure which had appeared at the foot of his bed.

"If you make a sound," I said, "I'll kill you. I may have to kill you as it is, but I don't wish to do so unnecessarily."

"Who are you?" he gasped.

"Don't raise your voice above a whisper."

"Anyway, you've come to the wrong place," he said, breathing quickly. "I have no money in the house."

"What is in the safe behind the picture?" I asked, and I saw him start.

"Nothing," he said. "No money, only a few private papers."

"What is the code word?"

"I'll see you to blazes before I tell you," he exploded; but as I raised the revolver he shrank back.

"What is the code word?"

I saw his lips trembling, and I knew he was in a devil of a fright.

"Tank," he said huskily. "You'll find no money there I tell you."

Covering him with one hand, I pushed aside the picture and swung the dial. The thick door opened, and putting in my hand, I pulled out three bundles of letters. One glance told me that they were in different handwritings, but I had no time to sort them out, and dropped four parcels into my pocket—the fourth I took for luck.

"What are you doing?" he shrieked, his wrath getting the better of his fear, as he sprang out of bed.

Before he could open his mouth, I struck him, and he fell on to the floor with a groan.

"Shut up," I hissed, "you blackmailing toad!"

At that he looked up.

"And so you've been sent to get the letters. Who sent you—Dolly?"

"I haven't the pleasure of Dolly's acquaintance."

"Then it was Beryl."

"And Beryl," said I, "is as much a mystery to me."

"Then it must be Constance," he said. "By gad, I'll have you for this, my friend."

"Don't call me your friend, unless you want me to flog you," said I sternly; and backing away from him, unlocked the door, took out the key and inserted it in the outside of the lock. "If you make any trouble, I shall come back for you," said I. "I shall stand three minutes outside this door, and your first shout will be your last."

I stepped out of the door, locked it, and was out of the front door and half-way down the stairs before I realised that I was still wearing my mask. I stopped only to pull this off, then strolled boldly into the streets.

It was quite light now. So light that the position for me was a dangerous one. I had to pass Hyde Park Corner, where three policemen, a coffee-stall keeper, half a dozen taxi-men saw nothing unusual in the appearance of a man in evening-dress on his way home, but would instantly recognise me once a hue and cry was raised.

I did not take a cab from the stand, but waited until a "crawler" overtook me; then I jumped in and told him to drive me to the Hotel Cecil. I stopped him short in the Strand, and went by a back way to my own hotel. Going to my room, I changed out of my dress clothes into a lounge suit, and, to the porter's astonishment, I left the hotel an hour after I had gone in, for I had spent some time burning the two packages of letters which I did not want.

Who Constance was, and who was Dolly, I have never discovered. There is little doubt that Price Wold earned a comfortable competence by blackmailing girls whose letters fell into his hands. It so happened that Beryl had no money to give, which, in a way, was worse for her.

At a quarter to six I was in John Street, Adelphi, under Beryl's window. I whistled, and heard the window sash rise, and presently there came down the cord I had seen on the window ledge. To this I affixed the bundle of letters, tying them tightly, and gave the cord a jerk.

I watched the dangling bundle until it disappeared into the room. Presently Beryl's head came out and her eyes met mine. She said nothing, nor did I. But her little hand went to her red lips, and she threw me a kiss. I was very well rewarded.

And now I am no longer the Worst Man in the World from one woman's point of view. She sits knitting on the verandah which overlooks the green-grey seas. Sometimes I see her turn her head in my direction. Price Wold did not prosecute. He left the country the next day, himself fearing prosecution.

Beryl sometimes expresses her scepticism as to whether I have reformed.

"You know, this must cost an awful lot of money," she said yesterday, fingering the pearl necklace about her white throat, "and I am perfectly certain the money you have in the bank ought to be in somebody else's bank, dear."

"That may be, dear," said I, "but the pearl necklace is your very own. It is a wedding present, bought specially for you, with tainted money, I admit, but it was not my tainted money."

"What do you mean?" she asked, open-eyed.

"I found it in Wold's safe," I said. "There was a little card inside: 'To Beryl on her wedding day.' I thought I had better bring it along, for already I was harbouring matrimonial designs."

Edgar Wallace – A Short Biography

Richard Horatio Edgar Wallace was born on the 1st April 1875 at 7 Ashburnham Grove, Greenwich. His mother, Mary Jane "Polly" Richards was born into an Irish Catholic family in Liverpool in 1843 and had worked in theatres, both as an actress in bit-parts and as a stagehand and usherette, until she married a Merchant Navy Captain, Joseph Richards, in 1867. He too had been born into an Irish Catholic family in Liverpool. His father had also been a Captain in the Merchant Navy, and his mother's family had a marine background. Mary was eight months pregnant with Joseph's child when he died at sea, and it was once the child been born that she first turned to the stage, taking the stage name Polly Richards.

She joined the Marriott family theatre troupe in 1872. It was managed by Mrs. Alice Edgar, Richard Edgar, Grace Edgar, Adeline Edgar and Richard Horatio Edgar, Wallace's father. In late 1874 Mary and Richard Horatio Edgar had a brief sexual encounter at the party following a successful show, and she fell pregnant. Worried about the scandal which would ensue and fearing that she might forever lose her job at the troupe, she fabricated an obligation in Greenwich would detain her there for at least six months. She lived in a room in the boarding house on Ashburnham Grove until her son, Edgar, was born. She had already made preparations through her midwife for a couple to foster the child, and when Edgar was born the midwife presented her with Mrs Freeman. Her husband was a fishmonger at Billingsgate market and she already had ten children. She was happy to foster the child and for Polly to make frequent visits to see him in exchange for a small sum of money which Polly made from her work in the theatre troupe.

Wallace was now known as Richard Horatio Edgar Freeman, taking his father's forenames and his foster family's surname. Broadly speaking his childhood was a happy one. The Freemans looked after him lovingly and he had good friendships with his foster siblings, particularly Clara Freeman, twenty years his senior, who often looked after him as a child. After a few years Polly's finances tightened and she was no longer in a position to afford the fee she had been paying the Freemans. However, they had grown to love the young Wallace and opted to adopt him in order to keep him out of the workhouse. Polly could no longer visit him. George Freeman was keen to ensure that he had equal opportunities and did all he could to secure him an education at St. Alfege with St. Peter's, a Peckham boarding school. Despite his adoptive father's efforts, though, Wallace left the school aged twelve for truancy.

Instead he went to work and by the time he was fourteen or fifteen he had experience selling newspapers at Ludgate Circus, near Fleet Street, as a worker in a rubber factory, as a shoe shop assistant, as a milk delivery boy and as a ship's cook. He stole from the milk company which resulted in his dismissal, and in 1894 was engaged to a local girl from Deptford named Edith Anstree, though he broke this off and instead joined the Infantry. He adopted the name Edgar Wallace which he took from Lew Wallace, the author of *Ben-Hur*, and his medical record records a diminutive 33" chest and a stunted growth. his first posting was with the West Kent Regiment in South Africa in 1896, though he did not enjoy military life, arranging to be transferred to the Royal Army Medical Corps. Though this was a less strenuous job, it was also significantly less pleasant and so he again transferred to the Press Corps, which he found suited him far better.

He was in Cape Town in 1898 where he met Rudyard Kipling and was inspired to begin writing and publishing poetry and songs. His first collection of ballads, *The Mission that Failed!* and was enough of a success that in 1899 he paid his way out of the armed forces in order to turn to writing full time. His first work was as a war correspondent for Reuters who kept him in Africa to cover the Boer War, and then for the Daily Mail in 1900 and various other periodicals after that. It was while he was in South Africa that he met and married Ivy Maude Caldecott, who was 21 when they married in 1901, despite her Wesleyan missionary father's strong opposition to the union, for several reasons, one of which was that Wallace's writing was not turning quite the profit he had expected it would. *War and Other Poems* and *Writ in Barracks,* both published in 1900, had not proved as popular as his first collection. Eleanor Clare Hellier Wallace, their first child, died of meningitis in 1903 and, in rather deep debt, they returned to London. Wallace used his contacts with the Daily Mail to get work with them in London, electing to write detective novels as a means of making quick money.

Wallace met Polly, his birth mother, in 1903. He didn't remember her from his childhood as he had been too young when she became unable to visit, so it was as though they were meeting for the first time. She was sixty years old and terminally ill, living in abject poverty. She had come to Wallace seeking financial support, but he turned her away. She died in the Bradford Infirmary later that year. In 1904 he and Ivy had a son, Bryan. He was still writing and had completed his first thriller, *The Four Just Men*. Since nobody would publish it he resorted to setting up his own publishing company which he called Tallis Press and he published a serialised version of *The Four Just Men* in 1905. He received promotional assistance from the Daily Mail in which he ran a competition for entrants to guess the method of murder in the final chapter, with a prize of £1,000 for a correct guess. Although the paper's proprietor, Lord Alfred Harmsworth, refused Wallace the £1,000 prize money, Wallace persisted and went ahead with the competition, recklessly advertising on billboards and buses all over the country, hoping to expand his advertisements across the Empire. His worried colleagues at the Daily Mail managed to convince him to lower the prize money to £500, split into a first prize of £250, a second prize of £200 and a third of £50, but with the total cost of his advertisements nearing £2,000 he would need to sell £2,500 worth of copies before he could see any profit. He was confident that this could be achieved in just three months.

Though he had remarkable enthusiasm, it became clear that his managerial skills left a lot to be desired. It soon emerged that nowhere in the competition terms and conditions had he included a clause limiting the competition to one single winner; instead, any entrant with a winning answer was entitled to their corresponding prize money. Thus, if ten entrants guessed the first prize answer, the competition was obliged to pay each entrant £250. This error was only noticed after the competition had been closed and the solution had been printed in the final installment of the novel, meaning that not only was there no opportunity to write his way out of enormous financial obligation, but the entrants who had guessed correctly would by now have read the final chapter and know they had done so. £250 was an enormous amount of money to the average Edwardian family and those entitled to it were likely to make a lot of noise if they didn't receive their money. Despite this, Wallace's fist instinct was to attempt to ignore the issue entirely, even as he discovered that he initial calculations had been dramatically over-enthusiastic and it would take nearer to two years of continuous sales to break even at the initial cost of £2,500, let alone the new figure which included every correct guesser. Compounding the problem even further was the awful realisation that as sales continued throughout the initial three month period and Wallace approached the £2,500 break-even figure, new readers were still eligible to enter and guess correctly. Though it is unknown how much he eventually owed his readers, Lord Harmsworth found himself having to loan over £5,000 in order to protect the reputation of the newspaper, since 1906 had come around and there still hadn't been a list printed of all prize-winners. It was less a charitable act than one of a man anxious that the failure would reflect ill on his own paper. Wallace filed for bankruptcy shortly thereafter and as a token gesture to his creditors sold the rights to the novel to Sir George Newnes, a publisher and editor, for £75. In the midst of this chaos though, Wallace managed to write and published *Smithy*, which would become the first of a series of *Smithy* novels.

Following this fiascos Wallace was dismissed from the Daily Mail in 1907 when inaccuracies which were found in his reporting, resulting in libel cases being brought against the paper. That year he became the first reporter to be fired from the Daily Mail and was his awful reputation prevented him from finding work at any other papers. Despite all this, though, he travelled to the Congo Free State later that year and reported on the criminal treatment of the Congolese people by King Leopold II of Belgium and the Belgian rubber companies. Up to fifteen million Congolese were killed in various atrocities, and Wallace was asked to serialise stories based on his experiences for her penny magazine *Weekly Tale-Teller*. He and Ivy had another daughter, named Patricia, in 1908. Though his new work for *Weekly Tale-Teller* was bringing in some money, their financial situation was still dire and Ivy was occasionally forced to sell off her jewellery and possessions in order to pay for food. In 1911 his Congolese stories were published in a collection called *Sanders of the River*, which quickly became a bestseller. He would publish eleven more such collections featuring a total of 102 stories of adventure and tribal life set on the river Congo.

From 1908 he started to enjoy a revival of both his success and his reputation. The majority of his initial writing he sold outright in order to make money as quickly as possible and placate his creditors in the United Kingdom and South Africa, but as his success saw the reestablishment of his reputation he began to find work once again as a journalist, beginning in horse racing for the *Week-End*, the *Evening News* and then as an editor for the *Week-End Racing Supplement*. Following this success he started his own racing papers, *Bibury's* and *R. E. Walton's Weekly*, eventually buying his own racehorses and losing thousands gambling. His success was insufficient to support his newly extravagant lifestyle and his marriage began to fail in the light of his financial irresponsibility. He and Ivy had their last child together, Michael Blair Wallace, in 1916, and she filed for divorce in 1918 moving to Tunbridge Wells with her children.

Wallace began to fall for his secretary Ethel Violet King and they married in 1921, having a child, Penelope Wallace, in 1923, who would herself go on to become a successful crime writer. Wallace now began to take his career as a fiction writer more seriously, signing with Hodder and Stoughton in 1921. He now began to organize his contracts more carefully, arranging for royalties and properly organized promotions, run by people more business-minded than himself. He was marketed as the 'King of Thrillers' and they gave him the trademark image of a trilby, a cigarette holder and a yellow Rolls Royce.

He was truly prolific, capable not only of producing a 70,000 word novel in three days but of doing three novels in a row in such a manner. His publishers signed off on almost everything he wrote as soon as he turned it in, estimating that by 1928 one in four books being read at any time was written by Wallace, for alongside his famous thrillers he wrote variously in other genres, including but not limited to science fiction, non-fiction accounts of WWI which amounted to ten volumes and screen plays. Eventually he would reach the remarkable total of 170 novels, 18 stage plays and 957 short stories.

Wallace became chairman of the Press Club which to this day holds an annual Edgar Wallace Award, rewarding 'excellence in writing'. In 1923 he broadcasted a report on the Epsom Derby horse race for the British Broadcasting Company, making him the first ever radio sports correspondent. His ex-wife Ivy had suffered from breast cancer between 1923-1924, and it eventually killed her in 1926 despite a successful operation to remove a tumour the year before. He wrote the essay "The Canker in our Midst" in 1926 which dealt, aggressively and controversially, with the problem of paedophilia in show business, describing how children were unwittingly left open to sexual abuse, and linking paedophilia with homosexuality. Its tone has been described as "intolerant, blustering, kick-the-blighters-down-the-stairs". He was appointed chairman of the British Lion Film Corporation on the back of the success of *The Ringer* and on the agreement that he give British Lion first choice on all his future work. This contract gave him an annual salary and a large amount of stock with the company, along with a stipend on all British Lion production of his work and 10% of their annual profits. This extraordinary contract gave him annual earnings by 1929 of almost £50,000, or almost £2 million in 2014.

He now became an active figure in politics, entering the 1931 general election as a Liberal contestant in Blackpool, rejecting the current government in favour of free trade. He lost the election by over 33,000 votes and went to America in late 1931, once again deeply in debt after buying the *Sunday News* which closed six months later. In America he quickly found work as a script doctor for RKO Pictures, enjoying early success with the 1932 adaptation of *The Hound of the Baskervilles*. This success, along with that of the play *The Green Pack*, established his reputation in America and he was able to see his own work adapted for film, beginning with *The Four Just Men*. His most successful theatrical work, *On The Spot*, which explores the life of Al Capone, has been described as "arguably, in construction, dialogue, action, plot and resolution, still one of the finest and purest of 20th-century melodramas". These successes led to his assignation on RKO's "gorilla picture" which would become famous as King Kong in 1933.

He worked on the first draft though he was beginning to experience severe headaches which brought about a diagnosis of diabetes. Despite taking medication to address his condition, it deteriorated in a matter of days. His wife booked him passage home but soon heard that he had entered a coma and died of his condition and double pneumonia on the 7th of February 1932 in North Maple Drive, Beverly Hills. In his honour the bell at St. Bride's church on Fleet Street tolled for the duration of the morning while the flags flew at half-mast. He was buried near his home in England at Chalklands, Bourne End, in Buckinghamshire. Once again, at the time of his death he was in severe debt, mostly to racing bookkeepers, though these debts were settled within two years thanks to the enormous royalties his estate continued to receive from his contracts. His writing has been translated into 29 languages, and is considered one of the most important bodies of Colonial writing.

Edgar Wallace – A Concise Bibliography

African Novels
Sanders of the River (1911)

The People of the River (1911)
The River of Stars (1913)
Bosambo of the River (1914)
Bones (1915)
The Keepers of the King's Peace (1917)
Lieutenant Bones (1918)
Bones in London (1921)
Sandi the Kingmaker (1922)
Bones of the River (1923)
Sanders (1926)
Again Sanders (1928)

Four Just Men (Series)
The Four Just Men (1905)
The Council of Justice (1908)
The Just Men of Cordova (1917)
The Law of the Four Just Men (US title: Again the Three Just Men) (1921)
The Three Just Men (1926)
Again the Three Just Men (US title: The Law of the Three Just Men) (1929) a.k.a. Again the Three

Mr. J. G. Reeder (Series)
Room 13 (1924)
The Mind of Mr. J. G. Reeder (US title: The Murder Book of Mr. J. G. Reeder) (1925)
Terror Keep (1927)
Red Aces (1929)
The Guv'nor and Other Short Stories (US title: Mr. Reeder Returns) (1932)

Detective Sgt. (Inspector) Elk series
The Nine Bears or The Other Man or The Cheaters (1910)
revised as Silinski - Master Criminal (1930)
The Fellowship of the Frog (1925)
The Joker or The Colossus (1926)
The Twister (1928)
The India-Rubber Men (1929)
White Face (1930)

Educated Evans (Series)
Educated Evans (1924)
More Educated Evans (1926)
Good Evans (1927)

Smithy (Series)
Smithy (1905)
Smithy Abroad (1909)
Smithy and The Hun (1915)
Nobby or Smithy's Friend Nobby (1916)

Crime Novels

Angel Esquire (1908)
The Fourth Plague or Red Hand (1913)
Grey Timothy or Pallard the Punter (1913)
The Man Who Bought London (1915)
The Melody of Death (1915)
A Debt Discharged (1916)
The Tomb of T'Sin (1916)
The Secret House (1917)
The Clue of the Twisted Candle (1918)
Down under Donovan (1918)
The Man Who Knew (1918)
The Strange Lapses of Larry Loman (1918)
The Green Rust (1919)
Kate Plus Ten (1919)
The Daffodil Mystery or The Daffodil Murder (1920)
Jack O' Judgment (1920)
The Angel of Terror or The Destroying Angel (1922)
The Crimson Circle (1922)
Mr. Justice Maxwell or Take-A-Chance Anderson (1922)
The Valley of Ghosts (1922)
Captains of Souls (1923)
The Clue of the New Pin (1923)
The Green Archer (1923)
The Missing Million (1923)
The Dark Eyes of London or The Croakers (1924)
Double Dan or Diana of Kara-Kara (US Title) (1924)
The Face in the Night or The Diamond Men or The Ragged Princess (1924)
The Sinister Man (1924)
The Three Oak Mystery (1924)
The Blue Hand or Beyond Recall (1925)
The Daughters of the Night (1925)
The Gaunt Stranger or Police Work (1925) revised as The Ringer (1926)
A King by Night (1925)
The Strange Countess (1925)
The Avenger or The Hairy Arm (1926)
The Black Abbot (1926)
The Day of Uniting (1926)
The Door with Seven Locks (1926)
The Man from Morocco or Souls In Shadows or The Black (US Title) (1926)
The Million Dollar Story (1926)
The Northing Tramp or The Tramp (1926)
Penelope of the Polyantha (1926)
The Square Emerald or The Woman (1926)
The Terrible People or The Gallows' Hand (1926)
We Shall See! or The Gaol-Breakers (US Title) (1926)
The Yellow Snake or The Black Tenth (1926)
Big Foot (1927)
The Feathered Serpent or Inspector Wade or Inspector Wade and the Feathered Serpent (1927)

Flat 2 (1927)
The Forger or The Counterfeiter (1927)
Terror Keep (1927)
The Hand of Power or The Proud Sons of Ragusa (1927)
The Man Who Was Nobody (1927)
Number Six (1927)
The Squeaker or The Sign of the Leopard or The Squealer (US Title) (1927)
The Traitor's Gate (1927)
The Double (1928)
The Flying Squad (1928)
The Gunner or Gunman's Bluff (US Title) (1928)
Four Square Jane or The Fourth Square (1929)
The Golden Hades or Stamped In Gold or The Sinister Yellow Sign (1929)
The Green Ribbon (1929)
The Calendar (1930)
The Clue of the Silver Key or The Silver Key (1930)
The Lady of Ascot (1930)
The Devil Man or Sinister Street or Silver Steel
or The Life and Death of Charles Peace (1931)
The Man at the Carlton or The Mystery of Mary Grier (1931)
The Coat of Arms or The Arranways Mystery (1931)
On the Spot: Violence and Murder in Chicago (1931)
When the Gangs Came to London or Scotland Yard's Yankee Dick
or The Gangsters Come To London (1932)
The Frightened Lady or The Case of the Frightened Lady or Criminal At Large (1933)
The Green Pack (1933)
The Man Who Changed His Name (1935)
The Mouthpiece (1935)
Smoky Cell (1935)
The Table (1936)
Sanctuary Island (1936)

Other Novels
Captain Tatham of Tatham Island or Eve's Island or The Island of Galloping Gold (1909)
The Duke in the Suburbs (1909)
Private Selby (1912)
1925 - The Story of a Fatal Peace (1915)
Those Folk of Bulboro (1918)
The Book of all Power (1921)
Flying Fifty-five (1922)
The Books of Bart (1923)
Barbara on Her Own (1926)

Poetry Collections
The Mission That Failed (1898)
War and Other Poems (1900)
Writ In Barracks (1900)

Non-Fiction
Unofficial Despatches of the Anglo-Boer War (1901)
Famous Scottish Regiments (1914)
Field Marshal Sir John French (1914)
Heroes All: Gallant Deeds of the War (1914)
The Standard History of the War – Volumes 1 – 4 (1914)
Kitchener's Army and the Territorial Forces:
The Full Story of a Great Achievement (1915)
Vol. 2-4. War of the Nations (1915)
Vol. 5-7. War of the Nations (1916)
Vol. 8-9. War of the Nations (1917)
Famous Men and Battles of the British Empire (1917)
Tam of the Scouts (1918)
The Real Shell-Man: The Story of Chetwynd of Chilwell (1919)
People or Edgar Wallace by Himself (1926)
The Trial of Patrick Herbert Mahon (1928)
My Hollywood Diary (1932)

Screenplays
King Kong (1932, first draft of original screenplay, 110 pages) While the script was not used in its
entirety, much of it was retained for the final screenplay.
The Hound of the Baskervilles (1932, British film)
The Squeaker (1930, British film)
Prince Gabby (1929, British film)
Mark of the Frog (1928, American film)
The Valley of Ghosts (192

Short Story Collections
The Admirable Carfew (1914)
The Adventure of Heine (1917)
Tam O' the Scouts (1918)
The Fighting Scouts (1919)
Chick (1923)
The Black Avons (1925)
The Brigand (1927)
The Mixer (1927)
This England (1927)
The Orator (1928)
The Thief in the Night (1928)
Elegant Edward (1928)
The Lone House Mystery and Other Stories (1929)
The Governor of Chi-Foo (1929)
Again the Ringer The Ringer Returns (US Title) (1929)
The Big Four or Crooks of Society (1929)
The Black or Blackmailers I Have Foiled (1929)
The Cat-Burglar (1929)
Circumstantial Evidence (1929)
Fighting Snub Reilly (1929)

For Information Received (1929)
Forty-Eight Short Stories (1929)
Planetoid 127 and The Sweizer Pump (1929)
The Ghost of Down Hill & The Queen of Sheba's Belt (1929)
The Iron Grip (1929)
The Lady of Little Hell (1929)
The Little Green Man (1929)
The Prison-Breakers (1929)
The Reporter (1929)
Killer Kay (1930)
Mrs William Jones and Bill (1930)
Forty Eight Short Stories (George Newnes Limited ca. 1930)
The Stretelli Case and Other Mystery Stories (1930)
The Terror (1930)
The Lady Called Nita (1930)
Sergeant Sir Peter or Sergeant Dunn, C.I.D. (1932)
The Scotland Yard Book of Edgar Wallace (1932)
The Steward (1932)
Nig-Nog and other humorous stories (1934)
The Last Adventure (1934)
The Woman From the East (1934) Co-written By Robert George Curtis
The Edgar Wallace Reader of Mystery and Adventure (1943)
The Undisclosed Client (1963)

Other

King Kong, with Draycott M. Dell, (1933), 28 October 1933 Cinema Weekly

Plays

An African Millionaire (1904)
The Forest of Happy Dreams (1910)
Dolly Cutting Herself (1911)
The Manager's Dream (1914)
M'Lady (1921)
Double Dan (1926)
The Mystery of room 45 (1926)
A Perfect Gentleman (1927)
The Terror (1927)
Traitors Gate (1927)
The Lad (1928)
The Man Who Changed His Name (1928)
The Squeaker (1928)
The Calendar (1929)
Persons Unknown (1929)
The Ringer (1929)
The Mouthpiece (1930)
On the Spot (1930)
Smoky Cell (1930)
The Squeaker (1930)

To Oblige A Lady (1930)
The Case of the Frightened Lady (1931)
The Old Man (1931)
The Green Pack (1932)
The Table (1932)

www.ingramcontent.com/pod-product-compliance
Lightning Source LLC
Chambersburg PA
CBHW061458170626
46811CB00004B/1568